The
Princess
Club

Christy Fiction Series

Christy® Fiction Series

The Princess Club

Catherine Marshall
adapted by C. Archer

WORD *kids!*®

WORD PUBLISHING
Dallas·London·Vancouver·Melbourne

THE PRINCESS CLUB
Book Seven in the *Christy*® Fiction Series

Copyright © 1996
by the Estate of Catherine Marshall LeSourd

The *Christy*® Fiction Series is based on *Christy*®
by Catherine Marshall LeSourd © 1967
by Catherine Marshall LeSourd

The *Christy*® name and logo are officially registered
trademarks of the Estate of Catherine Marshall LeSourd

Managing Editor: Laura Minchew
Project Editor: Beverly Phillips

Library of Congress Cataloging-in-Publication Data

Archer, C. 1956–
    The Princess Club / Catherine Marshall ; adapted by C. Archer.
        p.   cm. — (Christy fiction series ; 7)
    "Word kids!"
    Summary: When three girls find gold at Cutter Gap and form an
exclusive organization, The Princess Club, Christy watches in dismay
as the community in which she teaches is transformed by greed and
envy.
    ISBN 0–8499–3958–5 (pbk.)
    [1. Wealth—Fiction 2. Teachers—Fiction. 3. Mountain life—
Fiction. 4. Christian life—Fiction.] I. Marshall, Catherine,
1914–1983. II. Title. III. Series : Archer, C., 1956–
Christy fiction series ; 7.
    PZ7.A6744Po 1996
    [Fic]—dc20   96–26806
                                                           CIP
                                                           AC

Printed in the United States of America

96 97 98 99 00 OPM 9 8 7 6 5 4 3 2 1

The Characters

CHRISTY RUDD HUDDLESTON, a nineteen-year-old girl.

CHRISTY'S STUDENTS:
    CREED ALLEN, age nine.
    LITTLE BURL ALLEN, age six.
    BESSIE COBURN, age twelve.
    WRAIGHT HOLT, age seventeen.
    LIZETTE HOLCOMBE, age nine.
    GEORGE O'TEALE, age nine.
    MOUNTIE O'TEALE, age ten.
    RUBY MAE MORRISON, age thirteen.
    CLARA SPENCER, age twelve.
    LUNDY TAYLOR, age seventeen.

GRANNY O'TEALE, a superstitious mountain woman. *(Great-grandmother of Christy's students Mountie and George.)*

DR. NEIL MACNEILL, the physician of the Cove.

ALICE HENDERSON, a Quaker missionary who started the mission at Cutter Gap.

DAVID GRANTLAND, the young minister.

IDA GRANTLAND, David's sister and the mission housekeeper.

GRADY HALLIDAY, a traveling photographer.

BEN PENTLAND, the mailman.

FAIRLIGHT SPENCER, a mountain woman.
JEB SPENCER, her husband.
  (*Parents of Christy's student Clara.*)

OZIAS HOLT, a mountain man.

NATHAN O'TEALE, father of Christy's students Mountie and George.

DUGGIN MORRISON, stepfather of Christy's student Ruby Mae.
MRS. MORRISON, Ruby Mae's mother.

LETY COBURN, a mountain woman.
KYLE COBURN, her husband.
  (*Parents of Christy's student Bessie.*)

BIRD'S-EYE TAYLOR, father of Christy's student Lundy.

PRINCE, black stallion donated to the mission.
PRINCE EGBERT, unwilling frog captive.
OLD THEO, crippled mule owned by the mission.
GOLDIE, mare belonging to Miss Alice Henderson.
CLANCY, mule owned by Grady Halliday.

❧ One ❧

Touch that frog, Clara Spencer, and you'll be covered with warts from head to toe!" Ruby Mae Morrison warned.

The two girls stood at the edge of Dead Man's Creek with their friend Bessie Coburn. It was a sparkling, warm afternoon, and the icy water burbled over their bare feet.

Clara rolled her eyes. "That ain't true about frogs, Ruby Mae. Miz Christy says frogs is amphi-bians. We're goin' to study 'em for science class. And I'm gonna catch me this here one for her to teach us with." She pointed to the fat green frog sitting on a boulder in the shallow creek, sunning itself happily.

Ruby Mae sighed. Sometimes Clara acted like the biggest know-it-all in Cutter Gap.

"Warts," Ruby Mae repeated firmly. "Hundreds of 'em. Granny O'Teale says they start on your nose first-off." She nudged Bessie. "Ain't that right, Bessie?"

Bessie watched as Clara took another careful step toward the frog. "'Member that fairy tale Miz Christy told us where the girl kisses a frog and he turns into a prince?"

"'Course I do. Anyways, you oughta be careful how far out you wade, Clara," Ruby Mae advised. "We ain't never been this far up the creek before."

Clara took a deep breath and lunged for the frog. She grabbed him with both hands. Then she slipped him into the deep pocket of her worn dress and returned to the bank.

"I'm a-callin' him Prince Egbert," she announced, peeking into her pocket.

"Can't call him Prince," Ruby Mae said. She picked up a smooth stone and flung it far down the rushing creek. "We already got ourselves a Prince, in case you forgot. And the mission's stallion is a whole lot purtier than any warty ol' frog."

"Prince *Egbert*," Clara repeated. "And he don't have warts, I'm tellin' you."

"Kiss him then," Ruby Mae challenged with a sly grin. "Prove it."

Clara lay back on the grass, her hands behind her head. "Don't need to kiss a frog, 'cause I don't want to be a princess. I'm a-goin' to be a doctor when I grow up. Just like Doc MacNeill."

Bessie groaned. "Gals can't be doctors, Clara. That's just plumb foolish."

"How about Miz Alice?" Clara sat up on her elbows. "She's got a bag full of herbs and medicines. And she births babies and fixes up broken bones and such, just like the doc."

Bessie joined Clara on the bank. "Well, I'm a-goin' to be a teacher, just like Miz Christy. Only in a much fancier school than ours. One with lots of books and pencils, and no hogs under the floor. And no bullies like Lundy Taylor, neither. All *my* students will behave nice and proper-like, with citified manners."

Ruby Mae turned to stare at her two friends. They were lying side by side on the grass, staring up at the sky. They looked alike, the two of them. They were both smaller than she was, with long blond hair. Of course, there were differences, too. Bessie had plump, rosy cheeks and a silly grin. Clara had a thinner face, with sensible brown eyes, like she was always fretting over something or other.

She usually was, too. Clara was a thinker. She was always asking how or why or when—questions that would make a normal person's head spin like a top.

Bessie, on the other hand, was more of a dreamer. She was the kind of girl who would forget her head if it wasn't attached.

Ruby Mae knew both girls leaned on her. After all, she was a year older, and that made her a whole year wiser. She was taller than they were, with long, curly red hair. If only she could get rid of her freckles, she figured she'd be just about perfect.

"Doctor Clara Spencer," Bessie said in a wishing kind of voice, "and Pro-fess-or Bessie Coburn."

Ruby Mae sighed. Of course, they were only twelve. They weren't so smart about the way the world worked.

"Hate to tell you, but you ain't a-goin' to be doctors or teachers or frog princesses," Ruby Mae said as she stooped to get another stone.

"Since when can you see the future, Ruby Mae?" Clara demanded.

"Only Granny O'Teale can see the future," Bessie said. "And that's if she's reading the innards of a squirrel on a full moon night."

"What I'm sayin' is, you need cash-money to get those highfalutin' jobs. 'Cause first you need your schoolin'." Ruby Mae tossed another rock upstream. "And in case you ain't noticed, we're just kinda short of cash-money."

"Still and all, Ruby Mae," Bessie said, "what do you want to be when you're all growed up? If'n you could be anything you wanted, I mean."

Ruby Mae didn't have to think for a second. "I'd be a mama in a big house in a big city, like Asheville. Maybe even Knoxville. And I'd have me a beautiful golden horse, the fastest in the world. And about twenty-seven kids. All of 'em little angels, mind you . . ."

"Not like their mama!" Clara teased.

"And a husband as handsome as . . ." Ruby Mae paused. "As handsome as the preacher and Doc MacNeill, all rolled up into one. Only he'd comb his hair more often than Doc does. And wear fancy clothes with no patches. He'd have the preacher's eyes. And the doctor's smile. And he'd have a voice like—"

"R-R-R-R-IBBIT!" cried the frog in Clara's pockct.

"Like Prince Egbert!" Clara exclaimed. She started to giggle. Before long, she and Bessie were rolling on the grass, laughing so hard tears came to their eyes.

Furious, Ruby Mae rushed up the bank. "Ain't funny!" she cried, grabbing for Clara's pocket. Prince Egbert popped out and made a flying leap. He landed on the edge of the bank, eyeing the girls suspiciously.

"You made me lose Prince Egbert!" Clara cried. "Now help me get him back, Ruby Mae Morrison, or I'll tell Miz Christy what you done!"

Ruby Mae sighed. "You stop laughin' at me, and I'll help you get your frog. Deal?"

"Deal."

Carefully the girls made their way toward the frog. But as soon as Clara reached for him, he hopped into the air. He landed on a big rock farther down the creek.

"Pretend you're huntin' squirrels," Bessie whispered as they made their way toward the rock. "Nice and slow and quiet-like."

"If we was huntin', my papa's hound would be doin' the hard work," Clara said.

"We need us a froghound," Ruby Mae joked. Bessie giggled, but Clara was still too mad to laugh.

"This time, we'll surround him," Clara advised as they waded closer. "When I say three, we grab him. I'll do the countin'. One, two, THREE!"

All three girls lunged for poor Prince Egbert. He took another leap and landed at the water's edge underneath a thick, overhanging bush. Ruby Mae reached down in a flash and scooped him up, along with some rocks and sand from the bottom of the creek.

She held him up, nose crinkled. "Hope you're satisfied," she said, depositing the frog into Clara's pocket. "I'll be covered with warts by morning."

Ruby Mae dropped the stones she'd scooped

up back into the water. As she started toward the bank, something sparkling on the bottom of the creek caught her eye.

Was it just the sun, bouncing off the water? Pieces of shiny metal? Maybe a belt buckle or some nails?

"Come on, Ruby Mae," Clara urged. "It's gettin' late. And I need to take Prince Egbert home and find a place to keep him till school tomorrow."

Ruby Mae bent down. The bottom of her dress was soaking wet. The icy water swirled around her legs.

She scooped up the shiny things into her hand. For a long time, she just stared at the handful of rocks.

"Confound it, Ruby Mae," Bessie whined in her high-pitched voice, "what *are* you a-starin' at?"

"Rocks," Ruby Mae whispered.

"Well, toss 'em, already. My papa'll whop me good if'n I'm late again for supper."

Slowly Ruby Mae smiled at her friends. "You don't understand. These here ain't just rocks. These is the most beautiful, purtiest, shiniest, amazin' rocks in the history of rocks!"

She held out her hand. The rocks glistened like tiny pieces of sun.

"Fiddlesticks, Ruby Mae," Bessie said. "Them's just creek rocks."

"That's where you're wrong," Ruby Mae

7

whispered. She could feel her heart leaping inside her like a kitten in a burlap sack. "These is creek rocks made of *gold!*"

For a moment, nobody spoke. The only sound was the musical babble of the creek.

Clara finally broke the silence. "Come here, Ruby Mae," she said. "Let me see those."

Ruby Mae waded over and held out her hand. Bessie and Clara bent close. Bessie held one of the golden stones between her fingers. Her mouth was hanging open.

"Sakes alive," she whispered, "I do believe this here is real gold!"

"But where did it come from?" Clara whispered. "I ain't never heard of no gold in these mountains. Coal and such, sure. But *gold?*"

"Who cares where it came from?" Ruby Mae felt like her smile might just be too big for her face. "Do you know what this means?"

Bessie nodded, eyes wide. "Means we found us some cash-money."

"Wrong, Bessie," Ruby Mae said. "It means we're rich! It means we don't have to kiss us a frog to become princesses!"

❧ TWO ❧

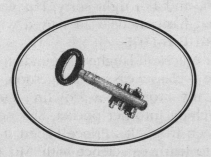

"Miz Christy! Miz Christy! The most amazin' and fantastic thing has happened!"

Christy Huddleston watched from the porch of the mission house as Ruby Mae, Bessie, and Clara sprinted across the field at high speed.

"What's gotten into them, I wonder?" Christy asked Doctor Neil MacNeill, who was staying for supper.

Doctor MacNeill ran his fingers through his unruly auburn hair. He was a big man, with a big grin to match. "With Ruby Mae and her gang, sometimes I'm afraid to ask."

The girls rushed up the wooden steps, panting for air. They were grinning from ear to ear.

"What on earth happened to you three?" Christy demanded. "You're all wet! And your hands are covered with mud! Do you realize you were supposed to be here half an hour ago to help set the table, Ruby Mae?"

"Yes'm, and I'm right sorry, but wait'll you hear what happened! It all started with—"

"R-R-R-I-B-B-I-T!"

Doctor MacNeill laughed. "Sounds to me like you have a classic case of indigestion, Clara."

"Ain't my stomach a-growlin', Doc," she said, reaching into her pocket. She pulled out a fat, green frog. "It's Prince Egbert. I got him for you to learn us science with, Miz Christy!"

Gingerly, Christy gave the frog a pat. She'd been living here in the Great Smoky Mountains for several months now, but she was still getting used to the wild creatures her students befriended. "That was very thoughtful, Clara. And a prince, no less!"

"And we," Ruby Mae added proudly, "are real, live princesses!"

"Well, you need to head inside, Your Royal Highness, and set the royal table," Christy said. "And Clara and Bessie, you two had better head for home before your parents start to worry. It's getting late."

Ruby Mae winked at her friends. "Don't need to set no table," she said. "From now on, I aim to just hire me a maid for doin' my chores."

"A maid?" Christy repeated, shaking her head.

Ruby Mae glanced over her shoulder. With a sly smile, she held out her fist and slowly

10

opened her fingers. "And here's how I aim to pay her!"

Christy and Doctor MacNeill exchanged a glance. Several small, damp yellow stones glistened in Ruby Mae's palm.

"That isn't . . ." Christy began. "I mean, it couldn't be . . ."

Doctor MacNeill picked up one of the stones. He held it between his thumb and index finger, squinting at it carefully.

"My, my," he murmured. "Where exactly did you find this, if you don't mind my asking?"

Clara cleared her throat. "Nothin' personal, Doctor," she answered, "but we all sort of agreed we'd keep that a secret between the three of us. You understand."

Just then, Miss Alice appeared in the doorway. "Ruby Mae!" she said sternly. "It's about time, young lady!"

Ruby Mae jumped at the sound of her name. Christy tried not to smile. Alice Henderson, a Quaker mission worker who had helped start the school, definitely had a way of commanding attention.

"Miz Alice," Ruby Mae said quickly, "you got to understand, somethin' mighty important's happened."

"I'm listening," said Miss Alice, tapping her foot.

"Me and Bessie and Clara is goin' to be richer than the king of England hisself!"

Miss Alice barely hid her smile. "You don't say?" Her eyes fell to the gold stone in the doctor's hand. She joined them on the porch.

"Neil? What's this all about?"

"Well, it seems our three little prospectors may just have found themselves some actual gold."

"So it *is* gold?" Clara asked. "Real, live, for-sure gold?"

The doctor shrugged. "I can't say absolutely, Clara. I've never actually held a gold nugget in my hand. But judging from the weight and color, I'd say—"

"We're rich!" Ruby screamed.

"We're a-goin' to be princesses!" Bessie cried.

"Who's a princess?" called David Grantland, the young minister at the mission, as he rode up to the house on Prince.

Ruby Mae ran over to greet the preacher and Prince. "We are," she announced.

Clara groaned. "Now, that does it for sure. Nobody else can know about the gold, 'ceptin' the people right here. Understand?" She glared at Ruby Mae.

"How come you're lookin' at me?" Ruby Mae demanded.

"Could be 'cause you got the biggest mouth this side o' Coldsprings Mountain," Bessie suggested.

"'Tain't true!" Ruby Mae cried.

Bessie rolled her eyes. "'Tis so."

"Ladies," David interrupted as he dismounted. "For the moment, let's set aside the question of Ruby Mae's communication skills. What's all this about?"

"The girls have discovered some very interesting rocks," Christy answered. "Neil thinks they might actually be gold nuggets."

The doctor passed the gold rock he'd been examining to David. "What do you think, Reverend?"

"Hmm. I had an uncle who was a collector of minerals and such. This definitely isn't 'fool's gold.' Pyrite's lighter and more brittle."

"I thought gold deposits were mostly out west," Christy said, "in California or Colorado—but Tennessee?"

"Gold has never been found in these parts before," said Miss Alice. "That's definitely a story I would have heard by now," she smiled, "a hundred times."

"Just 'cause it ain't been found here before don't mean this ain't gold," Ruby Mae said, sounding a bit worried.

David shook his head in disbelief. "I don't know how it got here, but this is gold, all right, Ruby Mae. As hard as it is for me to believe."

"Now that we know for certain, nobody more's got to know about this," Clara told her friends. "The preacher and the doc and Miz Christy and Miz Alice, well, they're the kind of folks can keep their mouths shut. But that's all can know."

"And Prince," Bessie added. "And Prince Egbert."

Clara nodded. "And our mas and pas. But that's it. Final. Right, Ruby Mae? That's what we promised each other on the way here."

Ruby Mae shrugged. "Don't see why we can't tell a *few* folks. Lordamercy, what's the point in bein' rich if'n you can't let folks know it?"

"I think Clara's right," Miss Alice said. "When the word gets out about this, this mountain cove is going to change overnight."

"Just like us," Bessie said dreamily. "Like plain ol' frogs turned into beautiful princesses."

"I fear it won't be anything quite that magical," Miss Alice said.

Christy could hear the concern in her voice. "What are you worried about, Miss Alice?"

"The same thing these mountains have seen way too much of. Feuds. Pain. Greed. Even death."

Ruby Mae held out her hand. The gold nuggets glistened like a wonderful promise. "Ain't no bad goin' to come from these," she said confidently. "We're havin' ourselves our very own fairy tale."

"I hope you're right, Ruby Mae," Christy said softly.

❧ Three ❧

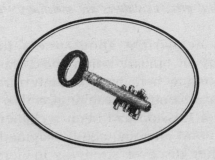

That evening, Christy ran a brush through her sun streaked hair and slipped into bed. She retrieved her diary and her fountain pen from her nightstand. Slowly she thumbed through the pages of the little leather-bound book.

She smiled wistfully when she looked at the very first entry:

> *. . . I have begun my great adventure this day, and although things have not gone exactly as I had hoped, I am still committed to my dream of teaching at the mission. . . .*

Farther down the page she read:

> *The truth is, I have not been this afraid before, or felt this alone and homesick. Leaving everyone I*

love was harder than I thought it would be. But I must be strong. I am at the start of a great adventure. And great adventures are sometimes scary.

She'd been right about one thing, that frosty day in January when she'd started her diary. Coming here had certainly turned out to be an adventure. Teaching at this desperately poor mission had been a challenge and a joy beyond anything she'd imagined. It had helped her discover strengths in herself she hadn't known were there.

She'd discovered love, too. Love for the beauty of these rugged, ageless mountains. Love for her friends and her students. And even the love of two very special men—Neil MacNeill and David Grantland.

But tonight, as she glanced over the pages filled with her careful writing, she felt strangely troubled. Christy looked across the room to her big trunk. Tucked inside of it was a little wooden jewelry box her mother had given her. And inside the box was a handful of stones. Golden, glittering, precious stones.

After some discussion, Ruby Mae, Bessie, and Clara had decided that their gold should stay at the mission house for safekeeping. Christy had offered to lock the stones up in her trunk until the gold could be deposited at the bank in El Pano.

Since the mountain road leading there had

been blocked by a recent rockslide, it could be awhile before anyone could get to the bank.

In the meantime, her wooden trunk was the closest thing the mission had to a safe. After all, everyone here was poor, and that included the staff at the mission. And this wasn't like Asheville, Christy's former home. In Cutter Gap, nobody locked their doors. Some people didn't even *have* a door.

Christy opened her diary to a fresh page.

I can't help but feel uneasy tonight. In a place as needy as Cutter Gap, the discovery of gold should be a wonderful blessing. But as Miss Alice pointed out, greed and envy can make people do strange things. I keep wondering how this will affect the children. I still remember how they looked at me that first day of school. Me, in my fancy patent leather shoes, when almost all the children were barefoot! "Silly, silly shoes," David called them. He was right, of course.

A soft knock at the door startled Christy from her writing.

"Come in," she called.

Ruby Mae, who lived at the mission, poked her head in the door. She was wearing her blue cotton nightgown. Her wild red hair was tied back with a ribbon Christy had given her. "Can I come in, Miz Christy?"

"It's late. You should be asleep, Ruby Mae. Tomorrow's a school day."

Ruby Mae leapt onto Christy's bed. "Can't sleep. I'm too excited about gettin' rich. I tried countin' sheep, but they kept turning into gold nuggets." She gazed at Christy's trunk longingly. "Can I see 'em one more time?"

"Ruby Mae . . ."

"Just a peek, I promise. I know it's crazy, but I keep fearin' they'll up and disappear. I mean, don't get me wrong, Miz Christy, I trust *you* and all. But it's like the only way I can believe in 'em is to look right at 'em with my own two eyes, you know?"

Christy set aside her diary. "All right. Just this once. But I'm not going to have a daily show for you and your friends. Understood?"

"Oh, no'm. Bessie and Clara won't let me tell anyone no how. My lips is glued tighter than a bear paw to a honey hive."

Christy retrieved the key to the trunk from her nightstand drawer. She opened the trunk, pulled out the small cedar jewelry box, and sat down on the bed next to Ruby Mae.

When Christy opened the box, Ruby Mae gasped. "Oh, my! They're even more beautiful than I remembered!"

"You just saw these gold nuggets a couple hours ago, Ruby Mae."

Ruby Mae picked up one of the stones.

"It's like these tiny little rocks have magic power. More than one of Granny O'Teale's herb potions, even. More than all the doc's medicines. This rock can make me into anything I want to be."

Christy started to argue that money couldn't buy happiness. That what mattered was that Ruby Mae be happy on the inside. That material things didn't matter.

But when she looked into Ruby Mae's shining brown eyes, she couldn't say a thing. Christy had grown up in a lovely home, with pretty dresses and fine food and loving parents and all the shoes she'd ever needed.

Not long ago, Ruby Mae had actually visited Christy's old home. Bessie had needed an operation at a hospital in Asheville, and Ruby Mae, Christy, David, and Doctor MacNeill had traveled there together. Christy could still remember the look on Ruby Mae's face when she'd first stepped into Christy's old bedroom. Seeing it through Ruby Mae's eyes, Christy had felt ashamed at the way she'd always taken her own good fortune for granted.

"Magic rocks," Ruby Mae repeated in a whisper. "That's what they is."

Christy touched the red ribbon in Ruby Mae's hair. "You know, that ribbon looks pretty in your hair," she said softly.

"Finest present I ever got," Ruby Mae

declared, still staring at the gold. "Practically the onliest one," she added with a smile.

Gently Christy put the gold nugget back in the box with the others.

"Miz Christy?" Ruby Mae asked thoughtfully. "You figure a gal from these here parts could ever make somethin' of herself? Maybe be a doctor or a teacher or have a passel of kids in a big city mansion?"

"I think a girl from these parts can do just about anything she sets her mind to, if she works hard at her schooling," Christy said, "and gets enough sleep." She placed the box back inside the trunk. "You head on to bed now."

"One more thing," Ruby Mae said when she got to the door.

"Yes, Ruby Mae?"

"I was wonderin' if you'd mind hidin' that key o' yours someplace more secret-like. I know I can trust everyone, but just in case . . ."

Christy stared at the brass key. She'd never bothered to lock her trunk before today. She eased the key into the lock and turned it until it clicked. Then she slipped the key under her mattress.

"How's that?" Christy asked.

"Much better. Now I can get me some sleep."

Christy sighed. "I hope I can say the same for myself."

❧ Four ❧

Now, there are several differences between frogs and toads," Christy said the next afternoon in the schoolhouse.

Prince Egbert sat on her battered desk in a small wooden box Clara had borrowed from her father. It was nice, Christy realized, to have any kind of educational aid—even if it *was* just a disgruntled frog.

When Christy had first come to the mission school, she'd been shocked at the lack of supplies. There'd been no paper, no books, no pencils, no chalk. In the winter, there wasn't even enough heat.

It still amazed her that she had sixty-seven students of all ages and abilities. Some could read and do math. Some couldn't even hold a pencil. And no matter what their grade level, they were all crowded into one tiny schoolhouse—a school that doubled as the church on Sundays.

On a hot, sunny day like today, it was especially hard to control so many children. It didn't help one bit that Ruby May, Bessie, and Clara had been disrupting class all morning with giggles and whispers.

Creed Allen, a mischievous nine-year-old, waved his hand frantically. "Teacher!" he called. "I got me a question about that there frog!"

"Yes, Creed?"

"How come Clara Spencer gets to bring her pet to school, but I can't bring Scalawag?"

Christy sighed tolerantly. Scalawag was Creed's pet raccoon. She'd made his acquaintance on the first day of school, when Creed had hidden the animal in his desk.

"This frog—" Christy began.

"Prince Egbert," Clara interjected.

"Excuse me. Prince Egbert," Christy continued, "is here as part of our science class, Creed. We're learning about amphibians, and—"

"But Scalawag's got manners to spare compared to that slimy ol' frog," Creed persisted.

"I'm sure he does, Creed. But he's such an entertaining fellow that we'd never get any learning done with Scalawag around, don't you think?"

"I s'pose," Creed said crankily. "But he's a

heap more good for learnin' than some warty fibian."

"Amphibian," Christy corrected. "And that brings me to an interesting point. Who can tell me the difference between a frog's skin and a toad's?"

"Tell you this," came a loud voice from the back of the room. "Ruby Mae's got more warts than either of 'em!"

"That will be enough, Lundy," Christy said firmly. At seventeen, Lundy Taylor was the oldest boy in school. He was also the source of most trouble. He was a vicious bully, and although he'd been better behaved lately, Christy never let her guard down around Lundy.

"Shut up, Lundy Taylor!" Ruby Mae shot back. She jutted her chin. "I'm better 'n you every which way there is. 'Specially 'cause now I'm a-goin' to be stinkin' r—"

"Hush, Ruby Mae!" Clara elbowed her hard.

"Stinkin' is right," Lundy crowed. "You stink like them hogs under the schoolhouse. Only they smell better!"

Christy clapped her hands. "That will be quite enough," she said. She was beginning to wonder if she should have let the children have a longer lunch break. The way things were turning out, it was going to be a long afternoon.

"Lizette?" Christy said. "Can you answer my

question about the difference between frogs and toads?"

Lizette Holcombe shrugged. "Nope," she grumbled.

Christy was surprised at her tone of voice. Lizette was one of her best students. "Is something wrong, Lizette?"

Lizette glared at Ruby Mae and her friends. "Nothin's wrong."

"Are you sure?" Christy asked gently.

"Why don't you just ask the *princesses* to answer? They think they're so smart. But you could take all the brains they've got, put them in a goose quill and blow 'em in a bedbug's eye!"

Christy knelt by Lizette's side. She was a tall, pretty girl, with long brown hair. But her face was splotched and red, as if she'd been crying.

"What's wrong, Lizette? What do you mean, 'princesses'?"

Christy feared she knew all too well what the answer was going to be.

"Ruby Mae and Clara and Bessie," Lizette said. "They started them up a club for princesses and such."

"Ruby Mae?" Christy asked sternly. "What's this about a club?"

Ruby Mae grinned. "We started us a club during the break. We're callin' it 'The Princess Club.' Nobody but me and Bessie and Clara can get in. It's glue-sive."

"I believe you mean *exclusive*," Christy said. "Did it ever occur to you girls that you might be hurting other people's feelings?"

"It's for their own good, Miz Christy," Clara explained in a reasonable voice. "We have our secret, after all." She gave Christy a knowing smile.

"You can have your dumb old secret," Lizette muttered. "You three have been carrying on all day like you've gone plumb crazy."

"Ain't crazy," Clara said. "We do have a secret. A gigantic secret."

"Big deal."

"A real big deal," Bessie said.

"Just ignore her," Clara advised. "She's just jealous."

"'Course, she'd be lots more jealous if'n she knew we found us some gold!" Ruby Mae cried.

Suddenly the room went still. Ruby Mae slapped her hand to her mouth. Bessie's jaw dropped open. Clara groaned.

"It's just as I said, Ruby Mae. You've got the biggest mouth this side of Coldsprings Mountain," Bessie hissed.

Ruby Mae's cheeks flared. The rest of the class stared at her in stunned disbelief.

"Well, it don't rightly matter if'n I told, anyhow," she said. "As long as I don't say where we found it or where it's hid, what harm is there in tellin'?"

"What do you mean, you found gold?"

Lizette demanded. "There ain't no gold in these mountains."

Lundy jumped to his feet. "You oughta whop her good for tellin' lies, Teacher!"

"If'n you found real live gold," Creed cried, "show it to us, Ruby Mae! That's a heap more edu-cational than that ol' frog!"

Instantly, the class erupted into shouts and jeers. Christy clapped her hands to get their attention, but it was no use.

In desperation, she climbed onto her chair. She tried yelling. She tried waving. When nothing else worked, she decided to try a trick David, who taught math and Bible study, had shown her. She put two fingers in her mouth and let out an ear-splitting whistle.

At last, the room quieted. "Wow, Teacher," Creed said in an awed voice, "you whistle better than a feller!"

"Sit down, everybody," Christy instructed as she climbed off her chair. "Now, I want one thing made clear. This is a place where we are all equal, and we are all here to learn."

"But Teacher," asked Mountie O'Teale, a shy ten-year-old, "is it really true they're rich?"

Christy put her hands on her hips. Now that Ruby Mae had let the cat out of the bag, she couldn't lie.

"It's true that Ruby Mae and her friends found some interesting stones that are prob-ably gold." Her words caused a fresh gasp from the class. "But that is their business, and I do not want it to be part of the discussion in this classroom. As a matter of fact, I do not want to hear anyone uttering the words 'gold' or 'rich' or 'club' in this class."

"I thought only cows had udders, Teacher," Creed said.

"I meant 'don't talk about these things,' Creed," Christy said. "And while we're at it, the only princesses I want to hear about are in fairy tales. Understood?"

She looked directly at Ruby Mae and her two friends. They nodded obediently.

"Now I believe, when we were interrupted, we were about to discuss the difference between frogs and toads," Christy said. She held up Prince Egbert. "To begin with, a frog has smooth skin and long limbs. Can anyone tell me any other differences? Creed? How about you?"

Creed didn't answer. He was staring at Ruby Mae and her friends, eyes wide.

Christy scanned the room. Not a single student was looking at her. All eyes were glued to the three smug "princesses," as if they really were royalty.

In a way, Christy realized suddenly, here in Cutter Gap, that's just what they were. From now on, nothing in her classroom would be the same.

❧ Five ❧

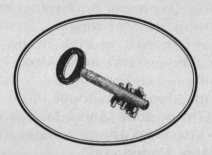

I now declare the first official meeting of The Princess Club is a-startin'," Ruby Mae announced after school.

The three girls were outside the small shed that David had built to house Prince; Goldie, Miss Alice's palomino mare; and Old Theo, the mule. Ruby Mae was carefully brushing Prince's glossy flanks. Clara was scratching his ears. And Bessie was feeding him a carrot from Miss Ida's vegetable garden.

"Before we start," Clara said in a whisper, "check all around to make sure we wasn't followed."

"Don't be a fool, Clara." Ruby Mae rolled her eyes. "Ain't nobody followin' us. You're actin' jittery as a squirrel with a hungry hound on his tail."

"Wouldn't need to," Clara shot back, "if'n

you coulda kept your mouth shut. I heard Lundy talkin' after school, sayin' how he was going to figure out where we found the gold and get some of his own."

Bessie gulped. "And you know Lundy. He'd as soon steal it as find it his own self."

"Listen here, you two lily-livers." Ruby Mae could tell she was going to have to be stern with her friends if she wanted any peace. "People was goin' to find out about the gold, one way or the other. You told your parents, right?"

Both girls nodded.

"Well, how long do you think a secret like that's goin' to keep here in the Cove?" She moved to Prince's other side and began brushing his silky mane. "Remember that time Violet McKnapp run off with Elroy Smith to get hitched? Remember how she only told Mary Allen and made her promise not to tell a soul?"

"Yep," Bessie said.

"Well, how long do you figure *that* secret lasted? A day, maybe two? *Our* secret is a whole lot bigger than Violet's."

"I s'pose you're right," Bessie admitted. "It's plumb unnatural for a secret like ours to stay a secret. People bein' how they is."

"And people's mouths bein' as big as they is," Clara added, glaring at Ruby Mae.

"There ain't no use snifflin' about spilled milk." Ruby Mae set down her brush and gave Prince a hug. "Besides, we got things to talk about. Princess Club things."

Ruby Mae hopped onto the slat fence and motioned for the others to join her. "Let's do our meetin' here. Nice and proper-like."

"I ain't never been a member in an actual club before," Bessie said excitedly.

"You ain't never had a reason to be special before," Ruby Mae pointed out.

Clara cleared her throat. "I think the first thing we should do is figure out what we're a-goin' to do with the gold. Pa says we got to take it to the bank and split it up three ways, nice and fair, Morrisons and Spencers and Coburns. But part of the road to El Pano's blocked by a rockslide. That's why Mr. Pentland hasn't brought mail in so long. So it'll likely be awhile before we can go to the bank."

"It'll be fine with Miz Christy," Ruby Mae said. "'Course, I'd feel better if'n it was in a nice, safe bank."

"I think Pa wants to build us a better house with the cash-money," Clara said. "Maybe one with real floors instead of dirt."

Ruby Mae nodded. "It's true the grown-ups will have their own ideas about what to do with all the cash-money. But I figure we found it, so we oughta get to spend some of it. Besides, there'll be plenty to go around."

"I want to buy me a dress all frilly and

puffy, with silk ribbons," Bessie said in a far-away voice.

"And I want to get me a horse of my own," Ruby Mae said. "I love Prince, but I got to share him with the preacher. My horse'll be the color of gold, with a white star on his head. And faster than the wind!"

"And I want—" Suddenly Clara stopped. The sound of someone whistling floated on the air. "Everyone hush!" she instructed.

"It might be Lundy, or one of the other big boys, come to find out about the gold," Bessie whispered.

"I told you we should have made sure we weren't followed!" Clara said. "People get mighty greedy when they hear the word 'gold.'"

Just then, a lone figure emerged from the woods. He had a large belly and a red beard. On his back, the man carried a strange-looking black contraption with long wooden legs. Behind him trudged a gray mule laden with packs. The mule seemed to be limping.

When the man noticed the girls, he waved and turned in their direction.

"Wonder what a stranger's doin' in these parts," Bessie murmured.

"Flatlander, I'll bet," Clara said. "He looks lost. Whatever you do," she added under her breath, "not a word about the gold, Ruby Mae Morrison!"

"I ain't entirely feeble-minded, thank you kindly," Ruby Mae snapped.

"Ho, young ladies!" the man called as he neared. "What luck to find you. Where exactly am I, if you don't mind my asking?" He wiped his brow with a white handkerchief. "I'm ashamed to admit it, but I haven't the foggiest idea."

"Lordamercy, you must be lost!" Ruby Mae exclaimed.

"Most folks who end up in Cutter Gap aim to come here on purpose," Clara added. "Or they was born here and don't know no way to get out."

"Cutter Gap," the man repeated, chuckling. "Well, I'll be." He patted his mule on the head. "Seems we're a bit lost, Clancy, old fellow."

"It's easy to get lost in the mountains if you're a city fellow," Bessie said kindly.

The man pointed to the mission house. "And whose house might that be?"

"That's the mission house," Bessie said. "So I s'pose it belongs to the Lord, in a manner of speakin'. But He's lettin' Miz Christy and Miz Ida borrow it."

"You suppose I might find a bite to eat there? Clancy and I have been wandering these lovely mountains for weeks, and I haven't seen a home-cooked meal in all that time. He's pulled up lame, poor guy.

Slipped on a rock near a creek awhile back. Thought he was better, but he's been favoring that hind foot today."

"Creek?" Ruby Mae asked.

"Up on the west face of that mountain," he said, pointing past Ruby Mae's shoulder. "By the way, name's Grady Halliday."

"I'm Ruby Mae, and this here's Bessie and Clara."

"What's that strange thingamajig you're carryin'?" Clara asked.

"This, my dear, is a camera. The finest made. I'm a photographer by trade."

Bessie frowned. "You mean a picture-taker?"

"Indeed. Although I don't take pictures of people. Not anymore."

"What else is there?" Clara asked.

Mr. Halliday swept his hand through the air. "Why, all this, my dear. Nature itself. These grand mountains. These majestic trees. Flowers. Streams. Rocks."

"You take pictures of rocks?" Ruby Mae cried. "I never heard of such a plumb fool thing!"

"Yes, it is a foolish occupation," Mr. Halliday agreed. "Which is probably why I'm such a happy man."

"You say you've been up in the mountains for weeks?" Clara asked.

"Took a little longer than I'd planned," Mr. Halliday said. He pursed his lips. "Got a little

33

sidetracked, looking for something . . . important. But as they say, fortune is fickle . . ."

"Can't say as I understand your meanin'," Ruby Mae said, scratching her head.

Mr. Halliday shrugged. "No matter. Now, if you'll provide the introductions, I'd be most appreciative if you could escort me to the mission house."

"I'll feed Prince," Ruby Mae said. "You all go on ahead. It's almost time for supper."

Mr. Halliday nodded. "So nice to make your acquaintance, Ruby Mae."

Ruby Mae watched as Bessie and Clara, who were staying for supper, led Mr. Halliday to the mission house. She wondered what it was he'd been looking for, up there in the woods. She wondered where Clancy had gone lame. Could it have been near Dead Man's Creek?

"Nice to make your acquaintance," he'd said. Fancy talk, when a simple good-bye would have done just fine.

He seemed nice enough, but Ruby Mae couldn't shake the uneasy feeling that she was going to be very sorry to have made Mr. Halliday's acquaintance.

❧ Six ❧

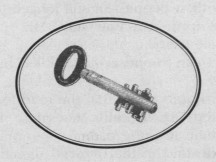

"My, my, I never dreamed when I happened upon your mission house that I'd be met with such a welcoming committee!" Mr. Halliday exclaimed as he settled into a chair in the parlor two hours later. "And I must say again, that was the finest piece of apple pie I've ever had the pleasure of devouring!"

Miss Ida, David's sister, handed him a cup of tea. "It's an honor to have you as a visitor, Mr. Halliday."

"Miss Ida's right," Christy said. "Imagine us hosting a man who's photographed the Wright brothers and Ty Cobb and even President Taft himself!"

"No longer, Christy. My professional days are past. I met many interesting folks along the way. A few scoundrels, too, come to think of it. I worked hard and made plenty of money. Now I take the photographs *I* want to take. Mountains are much more interesting subjects than people. Sit still longer, too."

"How long can you stay, Mr. Halliday?" Miss Alice asked.

"Oh, I can't impose. Just until Clancy heals up."

"You should know that the road to El Pano is blocked," David said. "Rockslide. Happens all the time in these parts."

"I'm headed in that general direction," Mr. Halliday said. "But I don't mind a detour or two. I enjoy stopping here and there to say hello. People around these parts strike me as the salt of the earth. Decent, kind. If a little shy."

"They are fine people," Miss Alice agreed, "despite their hard lives."

Mr. Halliday nodded sympathetically. There was a kindness about him that had made Christy instantly like him. Everyone seemed to like him, in fact—except, perhaps, Ruby Mae and her friends, who hardly said a word during supper. And now they seemed to have vanished from the house.

"I've encountered such poverty in these hills," Mr. Halliday said. "You have your work cut out for you."

"Poverty, but dignity, too," Christy said. "When I first came here, the hunger and ignorance and pain really frightened me. But then I started to see the goodness in these people."

"I'm sure life here can be very trying," Mr. Halliday said. "Living without hope is a hard thing indeed."

"Of course, hope can turn up in unlikely places," Christy said. "For example, the bottom of a creek."

"A creek, you say?"

"It seems Ruby Mae and the other girls you met came upon some gold nuggets the other day."

Mr. Halliday went very still. He cast a sharp glance at Christy. "Some . . . gold?" he repeated softly.

"We'd hoped to keep it quiet, but of course the whole Cove's abuzz with the news," Christy said.

"The prospect of that kind of wealth," Miss Alice added, "in a place like Cutter Gap—well, you can imagine the excitement it's kindled."

"Indeed," Mr. Halliday said.

David grinned. "Ruby Mae told me she hopes to buy a companion for our horse Prince."

"A friend for Prince?" Mr. Halliday echoed.

"She's quite the horse buff, you see."

"And Clara's even talking about going to medical school," Christy said. "Of course, their parents will have their own plans for the money."

Mr. Halliday set down his teacup. The china rattled slightly. "Yes," he said, "I imagine they would."

"Naturally, we're all curious as to where the gold came from," Miss Alice said. "After all, Tennessee isn't exactly known for its gold mining. And the nuggets had to come from somewhere."

Mr. Halliday nodded slowly. "Well," he said, "you know what the Bible says—'With God all things are possible.'" His voice trailed off.

"It's quite possible someone will still show up to claim the gold," David said. Then he shook his head. "But I'd certainly hate to be the one to deliver that news to Ruby Mae and her friends."

Mr. Halliday stared out the window, stroking his beard. For the first time since his arrival, he'd fallen silent.

"Mr. Halliday?" Christy asked.

"Hmm?"

"Are you feeling all right?"

Mr. Halliday waved his hand. "Of course. Just a little tired, after all my wandering."

For a moment, Christy wondered if she should have mentioned anything to Mr. Halliday about the gold. Something about the sharp way he'd looked at her made her uneasy . . . especially since the nuggets were hidden right here in the mission house.

On the other hand, he was bound to hear about them, anyway. If he was going to be staying here at the mission, Ruby Mae would tell him soon enough.

One thing was certain. Christy was going

to feel much better when the gold was safely locked in that bank safe in El Pano.

She was a teacher, after all, not a banker.

~ ~ ~

From her perch on the stairs, Ruby Mae listened to the grownups talking in the parlor. Bessie and Clara sat on the stair below her. They'd been eavesdropping for what seemed like hours. And the more they listened, the more Ruby Mae wished they hadn't.

She had a bad feeling growing in her stomach faster than a spring weed. She didn't like bad feelings. And she didn't like feeling confused.

Mr. Halliday had been looking for something, he'd said.

Mr. Halliday had been near a rocky creek when Clancy had gone lame.

Mr. Halliday was the kind of man who might have lots of cash-money.

Maybe even gold.

Clara sighed loudly. "It just don't make any sense, Ruby Mae. If'n the gold belongs to Mr. Halliday, why didn't he just up and say something when Miz Christy told him about it just now?"

"Come to think of it, he did sound a little funny when she brought it up," Bessie said. Her eyes went wide. "I have an idea. . . ."

"Uh-oh," Ruby Mae said.

"Maybe he stole the gold, and that's why he can't own up to it!"

"Or maybe we're just imagining things," Ruby Mae said. "Maybe it ain't his gold at all."

"Still," Clara continued, "he could have been up near Dead Man's Creek. And he was lookin' for somethin'. It *is* kind of a . . . what's the word Miz Christy taught us? A coincidence."

"He had his chance to claim the gold just now," Ruby Mae argued. She hated it when Clara got to thinking too much.

"Maybe you're right," Clara said, chewing on a fingernail thoughtfully.

"'Course I'm right."

"So then where *did* the gold come from?" Clara asked.

"You heard Mr. Halliday. Maybe God put it there for us to find. Like a miracle. You don't go askin' questions about miracles, Clara. You just say 'Thank you kindly' and feel mighty grateful."

"How come you happen to know so much about miracles?" Bessie asked.

"Because I been prayin' for one my whole life, that's how come." Ruby Mae stood, brushing off her dress. "Besides, it don't matter who the gold used to belong to. It's ours now. Finders, keepers. That's the rule."

"Finders, keepers," Clara repeated, as if she were trying to convince herself.

"Trust me," Ruby Mae said. "That gold was meant for us to have."

❧ Seven ❧

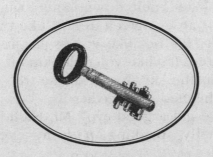

When Ruby Mae went down to breakfast the next morning, she was surprised to find Mr. Halliday sitting in the parlor, staring down at the floor. Photographs lay at his feet like a strange, patchwork carpet.

"Good morning, Ruby Mae!" Mr. Halliday said cheerfully.

"Did you take *all* these pictures?" Ruby Mae asked in amazement.

"Oh, this is just the tip of the iceberg." Mr. Halliday hooked his thumbs in his suspenders, contemplating the floor. "I was just trying to sort the wheat from the chaff, if you know what I mean."

"Can't say as I do."

"It means I'm trying to pick out the good photographs from the not-so-good ones. There are things to consider, like composition.

That's the way the parts of a picture all fit together."

Ruby Mae knelt down. She examined a picture of an evergreen tree. "I like this one," she said. "It's not like you're just lookin' at any ol' tree. It's like you're lookin' at the tree and up at the sky, too. Like the tree and the sky are hitched up together."

"You've got a good eye," Mr. Halliday said.

"Factually speaking, *both* my eyes work just fine."

Mr. Halliday gave a hearty laugh. "No, no. That's a way of saying you look at the world like an artist."

"I don't mind drawin'," Ruby Mae said, moving to another picture of a waterfall, "when Miz Christy's got pencils and paper for us, which ain't often. But truth to tell, I'd rather be ridin'."

"Ah, yes. The reverend mentioned you're quite an avid horsewoman." Mr. Halliday paused, as if he were about to say something, then seemed to reconsider.

"Ruby Mae!" Miss Ida called from the kitchen.

Ruby Mae stood. "Well, I got to go set the table for breakfast or Miss Ida'll have my head." As she turned to leave, she noticed a fat book near Mr. Halliday's chair. "What's that? I ain't never seen such a big book before!"

"That," Mr. Halliday replied, "is the Sears

Roebuck catalog. I was thumbing through it for supplies. You've never seen it before?"

Ruby Mae shook her head.

"Here. Take a look. It's chock-full of interesting things. Some useful. Some not." Mr. Halliday passed the book to Ruby Mae. "It's a catalog. That means you find things in it you want, and then you order them. A few weeks later, the item is mailed back to you."

"If'n you have cash-money," Ruby Mae said softly.

Mr. Halliday nodded. "Yes. That's how it works, all right."

Ruby Mae turned the crisp pages one by one. Hats and plows and hammers and shoes! Drawing after drawing of the most amazing things! It was like going to the general store in El Pano, only with a hundred times more shelves.

"It's like the world's biggest store," she marveled.

"Yes, I suppose in a way it is."

"Ruby Mae!" Miss Ida called again. "You stop bothering Mr. Halliday and march on in here. Breakfast is almost ready."

Slowly, carefully, Ruby Mae closed the amazing book. "I have to go," she said, gazing longingly at the catalog as she handed it back to Mr. Halliday.

"Tell you what," he said, "why don't you borrow it for the day? I'm in no need of it."

"You mean keep the book? For a whole entire day?" Ruby Mae cried in disbelief. "Why, I'd be tickled to death! Thank you ever so kindly!"

Clutching the book tightly, Ruby Mae started for the kitchen. But she hadn't gone far before she paused.

"Mr. Halliday," she asked, "can it be that you would have money enough to just out and buy things from a book like this?"

Mr. Halliday looked up from the picture he was examining. "Some," he said. "Enough."

"What kind of things do you buy?"

"Oh, supplies, mostly. I have them sent on to the post office in the town where I'm heading next. Last order, I bought a canteen and a horse blanket for Clancy. Some handkerchiefs for me. Odds and ends."

"I guess you made all kind of cash-money," Ruby Mae said, trying to sound casual, "takin' pictures of powerful folks like the President."

"I suppose you could say I made a good living," Mr. Halliday said gently. "But more importantly, I got to experience wonderful things. Traveling the world. Meeting many different kinds of people."

"Princesses, even?"

"Princesses, presidents, working men, thieves."

Ruby Mae gulped. "Thieves?"

"A few." Mr. Halliday smiled. "They're not

44

as frightening as you might imagine. Just people like you and me, trying to get by. People who took the wrong fork in the road."

"Well, I'd best be getting on to the kitchen," Ruby Mae said quickly. "Thank you again for the catalog. I promise I'll take real good care of it."

"I trust you completely," Mr. Halliday said.

❧ Eight ❧

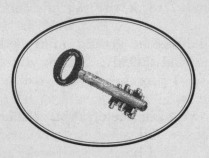

So, what do you think of our guest Mr. Halliday?" David asked that afternoon.

He sat beside Christy under a sprawling oak tree in front of the schoolhouse. It was the noon break—what the children called "the dinner spell." As usual, the students had broken off into small groups to eat. Some sat on the schoolhouse steps, but most lay on the wide blanket of green grass, soaking up the hot sun. A knot of children surrounded Ruby Mae, Bessie, and Clara. They'd become quite the celebrities, it seemed.

Christy unwrapped the sandwich Miss Ida had prepared for her that morning. "I like Mr. Halliday. What a fascinating life he must have had."

David gave a wistful nod. "Sometimes, when I hear talk of travels like his, I wonder if I'll stay in Cutter Gap forever."

"You're needed here, David," Christy said. "And being needed is a wonderful gift, don't you think?"

"Yes, I suppose it is." He reached for Christy's hand, then looked away shyly. "I guess we always want what we can't have, hmm?"

Christy wondered if David was referring to his recent proposal. She'd told him she wasn't ready to get married yet, and since then, things between them had been a little awkward. Perhaps it was because David thought Christy was really in love with Doctor MacNeill.

"Sometimes we don't really know what it is we want," she said softly.

David let go of her hand. He sighed, his dark eyes shining. "Maybe you're right."

"Are we talking about us?" Christy asked. "Or about Mr. Halliday?"

"Both. But let's stick with Mr. Halliday. He's a much safer topic." David managed a grin. "It's not his talk about knowing famous people that made me . . . well, a little envious. It was his freedom, I suppose. And the money he'd made. The things I could do for the mission, Christy, if only we had a little more money!"

"I know it sounds like Mr. Halliday's well off, but did you see the way he looked at me when I mentioned the gold the girls had found?"

"It's perfectly natural. Who wouldn't be intrigued?" he said, accepting the half sandwich

47

Christy offered him. "You know, it actually occurred to me that the gold might have belonged to him. I mean, *somebody* had to lose it. But I guess we may never know its true owner."

Suddenly, the tranquil air was filled with the sound of sobbing. Christy scanned the area. Near the schoolhouse, she noticed George and Mountie O'Teale together. Mountie was crying uncontrollably. George, her nine-year-old brother, was patting Mountie on the back, trying to comfort her.

Christy dropped her sandwich. "I just hope this isn't Lundy, up to his old tricks." Mountie was one of Lundy's favorite bullying targets.

Christy rushed to Mountie's side. "What's wrong, sweetheart?"

Mountie rubbed her eyes. "The p-p-p-princesses say I c-c-can't—" She stopped to take a gulp of air.

"Can't what?" Christy asked. She glanced over her shoulder at Ruby Mae and her friends. They were huddled over the Sears Roebuck catalog that Ruby Mae had borrowed from Mr. Halliday.

"The princesses say Mountie can't get herself a doll she set her sights on in that there book," George explained. He stroked Mountie's tangled hair. "Say she ain't got no gold. Say she's poor as a church mouse and they's rich folks now and that's that."

Christy wrapped her arms around the children. "Don't you listen to those girls. They aren't princesses. They're just Ruby Mae and Bessie and Clara, like they've always been."

Mountie sniffled, her sobs subsiding. "I-I knew I couldn't buy me the doll," she whispered. "I just wanted to *look* at her, Teacher. So later I could pretend in my head she was mine."

"You know what, Mountie?" Christy said, wiping the girl's dirty, tear-stained cheeks. "You can pretend right now. You don't need that picture. You can use your imagination to come up with the prettiest doll in the world. And when you're done, she'll be yours forever."

Mountie considered. "Just make her up, right here on the spot?"

"George will help you. What color eyes should she have?"

Mountie pursed her lips. "Blue, like George's. And sparkly."

"Good. And what color hair?"

"Just like Mountie's," George pronounced. "She's got right purty hair, even if'n it do have some tangles in it."

"There you go. Now you get the idea. I want you two to come up with the perfect doll for Mountie," Christy instructed. "Meantime, I'm going to have a little chat with Ruby Mae and her friends."

✵ Nine ✵

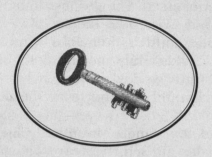

Christy marched across the lawn, hands on her hips. She shooed away the other children and led Ruby Mae, Bessie, and Clara into the empty schoolroom.

"Give me the catalog, Ruby Mae," Christy said as she sat at her desk.

"But, Miz Christy, Mr. Halliday said . . ."

"Now."

Reluctantly, Ruby Mae set the catalog on Christy's desk. "We was just plannin' on what we might could buy ourselves," she said in a pouty voice.

"I found me a dress with a puff-out skirt and a straw hat to match!" Bessie exclaimed.

"And I . . ." Clara began, but Christy held up her hand.

"Did it ever occur to you that your good fortune doesn't mean you can forget about your friends' feelings?" Christy asked. "Mountie was in tears just now because you told her she could never buy the doll she wanted. Why would you say something so cruel?"

"We weren't tryin' to be hurtful, Miz Christy," Clara said. "But she was gettin' so all-fired excited, lookin' at the doll picture . . ."

"We just didn't want her to get her hopes up," Bessie added. "I mean, just 'cause we found gold don't mean everybody in Cutter Gap's goin' to be rich."

Christy took a deep breath. She knew the girls weren't being deliberately thoughtless. But she had to put a stop to this before it got out of hand.

"Here's what you three need to understand," she said slowly. "Your good luck isn't a blessing at all if you end up making other people feel badly. You need to understand that there's going to be a certain amount of jealousy about the gold you found."

"Can't help it if'n folks got the envy in 'em," Ruby Mae declared.

"You can make it easier for them, though. These people are your friends, girls. That hasn't changed. Calling yourselves princesses, setting yourselves apart with a private club . . . well, that's just bound to make other people unhappy and angry. It's as if you're saying that because you may have more money, you're somehow better than they are. And that hurts."

Clara frowned. "We ain't sayin' we're better, Miz Christy. But the whole truth is, we are different now. Can't help it."

"But you can," Christy insisted. "You can be the same kind, generous, thoughtful friends you've always been. Have you forgotten the Golden Rule? How would you feel if Lizette and Mountie and George had found the gold instead of you?"

"'Tain't likely," Ruby Mae said, jutting her chin. "They ain't exactly bosom buddies."

"The *point* is, what if they had? What if Lizette had brought a catalog to school, full of things you might never be able to afford?"

Ruby Mae cocked her head. "I s'pose I'd be a mite jealous."

"Exactly," Christy said. "I realize you're excited about what's happened. But from now on, I want you to try as hard as you can to think about the feelings of your friends. Understood?"

"Yes'm," Clara said.

Bessie nodded.

"Can we still have The Princess Club," Ruby Mae asked hopefully, "if'n we do it private-like?"

"That's up to you," Christy said. "But I want you to think about how you'd feel if some of the other children wouldn't let you join their club."

"Speakin' factually, Miz Christy," Ruby Mae said with a sly grin, "you got us doin' so much thinkin' about other people, I don't see as how there'll be any room left for thinkin' about our 'rithmetic test."

Christy laughed. "Nice try, Ruby Mae."

⚊ ⚊ ⚊

That afternoon, after the children left school for the day, Christy sat at her desk, grading papers. The sun cast long yellow rays through the windows, spreading onto the floor like melted butter. The sweet smell of honeysuckle carried on the warm breeze. A scarlet tanager warbled joyously from the branch of a hickory tree.

Christy loved this time of day, when the echoes of the children's voices still lingered and the chalk dust still hung in the air. It was a time to reflect on her day. How could she help the children learn better? What could she do tomorrow and the next day to make their hard lives a little easier?

She scanned Ruby Mae's math test. Four wrong answers out of seven. No, Ruby Mae definitely did not have her mind on "'rithmetic" today.

Christy piled up the math tests and straightened her desk. She'd grade the rest at home this evening.

Before leaving, she opened her desk drawer and removed the Sears Roebuck catalog she'd put there for safekeeping. Locking up temptation, she thought with a rueful smile. Just like the gold in her trunk, back at the mission house.

She thumbed through the pages. Page after page of *things*. Things people needed, things people didn't need.

When she'd first come to Cutter Gap, she'd wondered how these people could get by on so little. She still remembered the first mountain home she'd seen—the cabin belonging to Clara Spencer and her family. It was gloomy and cramped, just two rooms, side by side. The family owned a few sticks of furniture and a big iron pot in the kitchen—a pot that was empty, more often than not. And yet the love and happiness Christy had discovered in the midst of those tiny rooms had filled her with awe.

Christy flipped to the back of the catalog, where she happened upon a page of school supplies. Chalkboards, pencils, paper by the pound, even beautiful desks! How wonderful it would be to be able to order everything she needed and have it all magically appear. But that was not the way the world worked— a lesson Mountie had learned only too well this afternoon.

"Knock, knock!"

Christy looked up in surprise to see Doctor MacNeill standing in the doorway. He was holding a slightly wilted handful of wild violets.

"Neil! What brings you here?"

"I had to stop by to talk to Miss Alice about a scarlet fever case she's been helping me with. Thought you might want to take a walk." He gave an embarrassed grin. "Sorry about the violets. It's the thought that counts."

Christy grinned. "I'm sure they were lovely."

"What's that?" Neil pointed to the catalog.

"Trouble, that's what it is."

As she started to close the catalog, Christy's gaze fell on a beautiful dress. Back home in Asheville, she'd seen one of her old friends in a dress just like it. Blue satin, sleeves trimmed in lace, tiny pearl buttons down the bodice. It had been beautiful.

Christy traced her finger over the drawing of the dress.

Be the belle of the ball! . . . the description began.

Quickly, she slapped the catalog shut. There was no point in imagining such a thing. It wouldn't be the same as having it.

Like an imaginary doll, she thought with sudden sadness.

❧ Ten ❧

For sure and certain nobody followed us?" Bessie asked for what had to be the hundredth time that afternoon.

"For sure and certain, Bessie," Ruby Mae said. She peered through the thick woods behind her though, just to be on the safe side. "Would you stop actin' like a scared rabbit?"

At the edge of Dead Man's Creek, the girls stopped to catch their breath. The dense greenery around them rustled with every breeze. The sun dappled the creek with sunlight.

"I could have swore I heard somebody a-whisperin'," Bessie said nervously.

"We doubled back just to be sure," Clara reminded her. She sat on the bank and let her dusty feet cool in the creek. "Even Lundy Taylor would have had himself a hard time followin' us."

"I still don't see why we had to come all the way back here with Prince Egbert," Bessie complained.

"Now that Miz Christy's done teachin' with him, we owe it to him to set him back in his rightful home," Clara said. "Could be he has a wife and kids, you know."

"Let's just get this over with," Ruby Mae said curtly. She didn't like coming back here any more than Bessie did. For some reason, returning to the spot where they'd found the gold made her feel guilty.

"You know, that talk about the gold with Miz Christy got me to feelin' kind of bad," Clara murmured as they walked along the bank.

"You've been usin' your head too much again," said Ruby Mae. "I can tell by the way your forehead gets all crinkled up."

"Ain't crinkled." Clara felt her forehead, just to be sure. "But all that talk about the Golden Rule and all . . ." She sighed. "This bein' princesses is awful complicated, ain't it?"

Bessie nodded. "Lizette wouldn't even talk to me this afternoon. You'd a thought I had the typhoid or somethin', the way she run off."

"And last night," Clara confided, "I heard my ma and pa arguin' out by the woodpile. Somethin' about how to spend the cash-money. My pa wants a new roof and a floor.

And my ma wants to save some of the money for later. My pa started to yellin', sayin' how are we even goin' to have a later if'n we don't have a roof over our heads? It was somethin' awful to hear."

"For a blessin'," Bessie said, "this gold sure is a passel of trouble." She paused. "What's that? Did you hear anything? Kind of a rustlin' noise?"

"You're imaginin' things," Ruby Mae said.

"All I'm sayin' is," Clara continued, "this gold sure does seem to bring out the argufyin' in people."

Suddenly, Ruby Mae stopped. A flash of white under some reeds by the edge of the creek caught her eye.

She bent down and fished her hand in the icy water.

It was a white handkerchief.

"What'd you find, Ruby Mae?" Clara asked.

Ruby Mae stared at the white clump of fabric in her palm. "Nothin' much. A man's handkerchief. Or maybe it's just a piece of fabric off'n a shirt. Can't rightly say."

The other girls joined her. "Can so say," Clara said. "That's a man's handkerchief for certain."

"It looks like the one Mr. Halliday was carryin' with him," Bessie said.

Ruby Mae wrung out the little piece of fabric. "Prob'ly lots of people carry handkerchiefs."

"Not in these here parts, they don't," Clara said. "Are you thinkin' what I'm thinkin'?"

"Not likely," Ruby Mae said. "You think more than a whole roomful of teachers and preachers put together, Clara Spencer."

Clara put her hands on her hips. "I'm thinkin' we were right about what we were sayin' before. I'm thinkin' that gold might just have belonged to Mr. Halliday. And I know you're thinkin' it too, Ruby Mae. Even if'n you don't *think* you're thinkin' it."

"Start over," Bessie said, scratching her head. "That's one 'thinkin' too many."

"What Clara means, Bessie," Ruby Mae said, dropping onto the mossy bank, "is that our gold may really be Mr. Halliday's gold."

"It's like one of them mystery stories Miz Christy reads us," Clara explained. "We've got us some clues, see. We know Mr. Halliday said he was lookin' for somethin' out here. We know he and Clancy were by a creek when Clancy slipped. We know Mr. Halliday's handkerchief was here. That's a lot o' clues, no matter how you look at it."

"'Ceptin' for one," Ruby Mae shot back. "Like I said already—how come he doesn't just claim the gold then?"

Clara shook her head. "I don't know why. I admit it don't make a whit of sense. But flatlanders ain't always as sensible as regular people. Them that comes from the city don't always know which way's up and which way's down."

"Maybe we should say somethin' to somebody," Bessie said.

"Why?" Ruby Mae demanded. "Mr. Halliday had his chance to claim the gold."

Bessie shrugged. "I don't know. It just sort of feels a little like stealin', Ruby Mae. And the preacher always says, 'Thou shalt not steal.'"

"He also says, 'finders, keepers.'"

"I ain't never heard him say that," Clara said.

"Well, if'n we asked him, he *would* say it, I'm pretty sure." Ruby Mae fingered the handkerchief. She didn't like this ugly feeling inside her, not one little bit. "Look," she pleaded, "even if'n it *is* Mr. Halliday's gold—and I ain't sayin' it is—I got to talkin' to him this mornin'. He's got plenty of cash-money. He told me he's met real, live princesses his own self. And presidents and rich folks. A few nuggets of gold won't matter to him one way or the other." She sighed. "Not the way they can matter to us. With that gold, we can make somethin' of ourselves."

"Maybe you're right," Bessie said.

"It's true he ain't said the gold's his," Clara conceded.

Ruby Mae slapped her thigh and stood up. "Exactly! Now, no more disagreein'. The Princess Club has got to stick together."

Clara held up her hand. "Here's the spot where we found Prince Egbert." She opened the box she'd been carrying and gently set it on its side. Prince Egbert hopped out, blinked, and looked up at the girls.

"Without you, we might never have found the gold," Clara said. "Thanks, Prince Egbert."

Just then, the trees behind them rustled.

"That ain't no breeze," Clara whispered darkly.

A branch cracked. A bush shook.

"There's somebody comin'!" Ruby Mae cried.

Out of the trees leapt Lundy Taylor. In his hand was a heavy rock.

"Well," he sneered, "if'n it ain't The Princess Club. Fancy the luck. Just so happens I'm lookin' to join up."

✺ Eleven ✺

Lundy took a step closer.

Standing higher up on the bank, he seemed to tower over the girls. He lifted the rock over his head. His black eyes gleamed.

"Tell me where you found the gold," he growled. "Right now."

Ruby Mae glanced at her friends. Both stood frozen in place. Bessie looked as if she were about to cry. Clara's eyes were darting here and there, searching for a way to escape. But Ruby Mae knew there was nowhere to run.

"I said, tell me where you found the gold, Ruby Mae!" Lundy shouted.

Ruby Mae could feel her heart thudding in her chest. She'd known Lundy Taylor her whole life. She'd listened to him sass Miz Christy. She'd watched him beat up boys half his size. She'd even seen him throw a rock at little Mountie O'Teale.

Lundy had done those things out of pure spite. There was no telling what he'd do for a chance to get rich.

"Ain't no more gold to be found, Lundy," Ruby Mae said. She barely recognized her own squeaking voice. "We done found it all."

"Liar!"

Lundy lurched down the bank toward Ruby Mae. She stumbled and fell in the shallow water at the edge of the creek.

"You tell me or I'll knock your head clean in two!" Lundy cried. He waved the big rock in front of Ruby Mae's face. "I'll do it, too! You know I will!"

"Stop it, Lundy!" Clara said. "Ruby Mae's tellin' the truth. We found the gold in this here creek, only there ain't no more to be had. We looked and looked ourselves already."

Lundy lowered the rock, taking in this new information. "Right here, in Dead Man's Creek?"

"Up there, just a few feet," Ruby Mae said, slowly getting to her feet.

"How do you know there ain't no more gold?"

"W—we don't," Ruby Mae stammered. "Not for sure and certain."

Lundy dipped in a bare foot at the creek's

edge and stirred up the rocks on the bottom. Then he bent down and scooped some into his palm, still clutching the big rock in his other hand.

"Don't believe you," he pronounced at last. "These is just creek rocks. Nothin' special about 'em." He scowled at Ruby Mae. "You're a-tryin' to put one over on me."

"No we ain't," Bessie said in a quavery voice. "It was just one of them things, Lundy. We was just plumb lucky, is all."

Lundy stood. Angrily, he slapped the rock in his palm. "How come you all get to be plumb lucky, and I get nothin'? That seem fair to you?"

"That's how luck is," Ruby Mae said with a helpless shrug. "It don't make a whit of sense."

She looked over her shoulder, trying to plot an escape. They could try running for it, but Lundy would be faster. He was bound to catch one of them. Ruby Mae was one of the fastest runners in school—faster even than a lot of the boys. She'd probably be able to get away. But she couldn't risk leaving her friends behind. If she had to stay and fight, she would. Three to one, they might just have a chance. If only they were closer to the mission, they could try calling for help. But out here, no one would hear them.

Lundy moved close to Ruby Mae, so close she could smell the tobacco on his breath.

"Tell me this, Princess Ruby Mae. What makes you so all-fired special you should get all that gold?" Again he raised the rock high. Its sharp edges glinted in the sun.

"I . . . I have an idea," Clara said suddenly. "S'posin' we give you some of the gold, sort of like a reward. For not hittin' us and all."

"Clara!" Ruby Mae moaned, but secretly she was relieved. After all, she wasn't going to enjoy the gold much if her head was split in two.

"A reward?" Lundy repeated. He stroked his stubbled chin.

Clara nodded. "Like for instance, s'posin' we give you a nugget of gold if'n you let us go?"

"Or even two?" Bessie added hopefully.

"Let's not get carried away," Ruby Mae muttered.

"That's an idea, all right," Lundy said, sounding reasonable at last.

"For starters," Ruby Mae said, "how about you just toss that silly ol' rock aside?"

Lundy thought for a minute. His face darkened. "I got me a better idea. How about you three princesses just tell me where the gold's hid and give it all to me? Or else I'll bash your royal heads in!"

Lundy grabbed a lock of Ruby Mae's hair and yanked her closer. She let out a scream of protest. Bessie began to sob.

With the rock inches from Ruby Mae's temple, Lundy smiled a dangerous smile.

"Well?" he said. "I'm gettin' tired of your games. Just tell me where the gold is. I'd hate to have to get blood all over that pretty hair of yours."

"Run, Bessie! Run, Clara!" Ruby Mae screamed. "Get help!"

"Ain't nowhere they can run in time to save your sorry head," Lundy said. "Now, tell me how I can get me that gold . . ."

"Let her go, Lundy!" A booming voice filled the air. "Now!"

Lundy released Ruby Mae's hair and spun around.

To her amazement, there on the bank stood Doctor MacNeill and Miz Christy.

In two strides, the doctor reached Lundy. Lundy tried to resist, but he was no match. The doctor pinned Lundy's arm behind his back. The rock fell to the ground.

"Lemme go!" Lundy moaned. "My arm! You're a-hurtin' my arm!"

"Hurts, you say?" the doctor inquired.

"Burns like fire!"

"I want you to remember this feeling, Lundy," the doctor said. "Because if I ever catch you near these girls again, it's going to hurt a whole lot worse. You get my meaning?"

Lundy nodded.

"I'm sorry. I didn't quite catch your answer."

"Yes!" Lundy squawked. "Yes!"

Slowly the doctor released him. Lundy rubbed his arm. "Docs ain't s'posed to go around hurtin' people," he muttered.

Doctor MacNeill shrugged. "I went to a very unorthodox medical school."

"What's that supposed to mean?" Lundy demanded. "You know I don't know no fancy words."

"It means," Christy said sharply, "that you'd better watch yourself from now on, Lundy."

Ruby Mae blinked in disbelief. She'd never heard Miz Christy sound so riled, not even that time Lundy had hit Mountie O'Teale.

"But they said I could have a re-ward," Lundy murmured, pointing at the girls.

"Well, they were mistaken," said Christy. "They don't have the gold in their possession."

"Who does?"

"It's safely locked away."

Lundy's eyes narrowed. "I bet you got it, Teacher-gal."

Doctor MacNeill took a step toward Lundy, who backed up instantly. "Apparently, I didn't make myself clear," the doctor said with quiet rage.

Lundy spit on the ground, glaring at Ruby Mae. "You won't be princesses much longer," he said. Then he turned and vanished into the trees.

Christy rushed to Ruby Mae's side and pulled her close. "Are you all right?"

"Fine and dandy," Ruby Mae reported. "Sure am glad you two happened along, though."

"We were looking for violets," Christy said. Her blue eyes were shimmering with tears. "We almost headed in the other direction, toward Stony Peak. When I think what might have happened if we hadn't been here . . ."

"We'd have figured somethin' out, Miz Christy," Ruby Mae said reassuringly.

Bessie sniffled loudly. "I ain't so sure about that, Ruby Mae."

"What's that?" Christy asked, pointing to the white handkerchief Ruby Mae was still clutching.

"This?" Ruby Mae stuffed the handkerchief in her pocket. "Nothin'. Just some ol' scrap of fabric we found by the bank."

Christy sighed. "I still can't get over how lucky it is we were in the right place at the right time."

"Well, it's over now," Ruby Mae said lightly. "The doc sure scared the daylights outa Lundy. He won't be botherin' us again. His bark's worse than his bite, anyhow."

Doctor MacNeill was gazing off in the direction Lundy had run. "Don't be too sure about Lundy Taylor, Ruby Mae. Gold can do strange things to people."

Ruby Mae started to argue, but the look on the doctor's face made her fall silent. She'd never seen that look before, not on the doc. Doc MacNeill wasn't afraid of anything.

And yet, right now, if she didn't know better, she'd have sworn he looked awfully worried. Maybe even scared.

❧ Twelve ❧

Grady Halliday," Christy said, "I'd like you to meet my dear friend, Fairlight Spencer, and her husband, Jeb."

"Pleased to make your acquaintance." Mr. Halliday shook hands with the Spencers. "Lovely morning for a church service. If a little on the hot side."

"I think you'll enjoy David's sermon," Christy said. "Church here in Cutter Gap isn't quite like anything you've ever seen before."

Mr. Halliday smiled. "I'm looking forward to it."

Christy surveyed the area outside the church. Knots of people stood here and there, chatting. Children and dogs chased each other in crazy circles. A group of men hovered near the entrance, chewing tobacco. Still, she couldn't help but notice there were a lot of faces missing.

"This is an unusually small turnout," Christy commented. "I wonder why?"

"Perhaps the fine weather is proving too tempting," Mr. Halliday suggested. He pulled a handkerchief from his pocket and wiped his brow.

"Something's temptin' them, all right," Fairlight said. Her lovely eyes sparkled. "But I'm guessin' it's not the weather."

"We passed Ozias Holt and Nathan O'Teale on the way here," Jeb said. "Both of 'em with shovels and picks. Said they didn't have time to look for the Lord." He shook his head. "Lookin' for gold instead."

"This gold discovery certainly seems to have had an effect on the community," Mr. Halliday said.

Fairlight sighed. "It's startin' to seem like a blessin' *and* a curse. Poor Clara ain't slept the last two nights, since Lundy Taylor went after the girls up by the creek. At first, I had such hopes about the gold . . . fixin' up the cabin, maybe. Or savin' for the children's schoolin'. But if it means my little Clara has to live in fear . . ."

"If I get my hands on Lundy, I'll show him a thing or two about fear," Jeb said gruffly, his hands clenched in anger.

Christy gazed at him sadly. It was only

natural for Jeb to want to protect his children. Still, he was usually such a gentle man. It hurt to see him so angry.

"I think Neil did a pretty good job of scaring Lundy Taylor, Jeb," she said, trying to sound reassuring. But she could see from his worried expression that he wasn't convinced.

They headed into the church. Even though the simple building served as Christy's schoolroom all week, it always felt fresh to her on Sunday. Maybe it was the hushed anticipation in the room. Maybe it was seeing David, dressed in his Sunday best—a dark suit, white shirt, and black tie. Maybe it was seeing the scrubbed faces and combed hair of her students, who were generally on their best behavior.

But Christy knew it was more than just those obvious things. The real reason the room felt changed was the feeling of joy and hope that filled the dusty, rough room like summer sunshine.

Today, though, as she settled into a pew with her friends, something was missing. The usual happy mood had been replaced by something much darker. People were grumbling, whispering, and pointing. Much of the attention seemed to focus on Ruby Mae, Bessie, and Clara, who were sitting together in a front pew.

A few rows behind them sat Kyle and Lety

Coburn, Bessie's parents. Next to the Coburns sat Duggin Morrison, Ruby Mae's stepfather, and his wife. Christy was surprised to see Duggin. He didn't come to church much. She imagined Ruby Mae was surprised to see him, too. She and her stepfather didn't get along well. That was one reason why Ruby Mae lived at the mission.

As soon as David cleared his throat, the room quieted. "It's nice to see all of you today," he began, "particularly since some seem to have gotten sidetracked en route by, shall we say, more earthly concerns—"

He was interrupted by some loud talk coming from the direction of Duggin's pew. Christy turned to see what the commotion was about. Bessie's father and Ruby Mae's stepfather seemed to be arguing about something.

"Gentlemen?" David said calmly.

"Er, sorry, Preacher," Kyle mumbled.

Christy smiled. By now, David had grown used to such interruptions. Two weeks ago, he'd had to suspend his sermon when a skunk had decided to join the congregation.

"Today," David continued, "I thought we'd reflect a bit on what it means to be wealthy in our society. Does it mean having a lot of material things? A nice home, perhaps even an automobile? Beautiful clothes? Money in the bank?"

"Ask them princesses, Preacher!" called a young voice. "They know all about bein' rich!"

That had to be Creed Allen, Christy thought, as the room exploded into laughter.

David laughed, too. "Thank you, Creed. You bring me to an interesting point. By now I suppose there's not a soul in Cutter Gap who hasn't heard about the intriguing discovery of some gold in these mountains. But is gold the way we measure true wealth? What about happiness? Love? What about the pride that comes from hard work? Which means more—a penny, earned by the honest sweat of your brow . . . or a dollar in ill-gotten gains?"

"Give me the dollar any ol' day!" someone cried.

Again, everyone laughed. But this time, Christy sensed tension in the air, too.

David waited until the room was perfectly still. Long moments passed. At last he spoke again.

"'What is a man profited,'" he said softly, "'if he shall gain the whole world, and lose his own soul?'"

His words hung in the air. Suddenly, Ruby Mae's stepfather leapt to his feet. "Is *so* more Ruby Mae's!" he screamed. "She's the one what found it!"

Bessie's father jumped up, fists raised.

"Wouldn't have found it a-tall, without my Bessie's frog!"

"Bessie's frog!" Clara cried in outrage. "Weren't Bessie's frog! Prince Egbert was *mine!* I'm the one oughta get more of the gold, if anyone does!"

"Clara!" Fairlight said in embarrassment. "You sit down this instant and apologize to the preacher!"

"But Ma—"

David held up a warning hand. "I think we all need—"

Wham! Duggin let loose with a powerful punch to Kyle's belly.

"Fight!" Creed yelped in glee, jumping onto a pew.

Kyle swung back wildly. After several tries, he connected with Duggin's nose. Blood trickled onto his dirty shirt.

Suddenly the whole room went crazy. Kyle and Duggin bumped into the benches, grunting as they threw punches at each other, most of which missed. Soon a few other men were drawn into the fight. Somebody threw a chair. Somebody else knocked over the blackboard. Two babies began to squall. In the corner, somebody was taking bets on who would win.

Into the fray ran Christy, David, Mr. Halliday, Jeb, and Fairlight. But before they could separate the combatants, Granny O'Teale appeared.

The tiny, frail woman stood in front of Kyle and Duggin, her cane poised over her head.

"Stop it, you pig-headed, greedy geezers," she commanded, "or I'll whop you both to kingdom come!"

Kyle and Duggin stopped in mid-swing. They looked at Granny and gulped. The rest of the room fell silent, too.

"Granny," David said, giving her a hug, "I couldn't have said it better myself!"

"My, my," Mr. Halliday whispered to Christy. "I see you weren't exaggerating before. This certainly is very different from any service I've ever attended!"

"It's usually a little calmer," Christy said with a weak smile. "I'm sorry you had to see this."

Mr. Halliday didn't answer. He seemed to be lost in thought. "You know, Christy," he said at last, "I'm sorry, too."

❧ Thirteen ❧

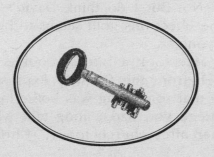

That afternoon, Christy was sitting in the yard writing a letter to her parents when Ruby Mae emerged from the mission house. She was carrying a napkin full of oatmeal cookies.

"For you," Ruby Mae said. "Miss Ida just made 'em."

"Thank you, Ruby Mae. I could use a little pick-me-up. After that fight at the church, I didn't have much appetite at noon."

"I brung some for Mr. Halliday, too."

"He's in the storage shed," Christy said. "We told him he could use it to develop his photographs." She put down her pen and paper, then reached for a cookie. "Come on. I'll walk over with you."

"That was quite a commotion at church today," Ruby Mae said as they started across the lawn. She paused. "You think the preacher was mad?"

"Mad? No. But I do think David's worried about the effect this gold seems to be having on everyone."

Ruby Mae took a bite of cookie. Christy could tell from the faraway expression on her face that something was bothering her.

"I noticed you had a long talk with your stepfather after church today," Christy said gently.

"My step-pa asked if maybe I wanted to come back home to live."

"Oh? What did you tell him?"

"I told him I was right happy livin' here at the mission house. And if'n I moved back home, it'd be such a long ways to school I might hardly never go."

"And what did he say?"

"Said that was all right with him. As long as I didn't get uppity and forget to honor my pa and ma and give them what's rightfully theirs."

"The gold?"

Ruby Mae nodded. "I told him how I maybe wanted to save the gold. You know, for the future. Told him all kinds of crazy dreams I have." She stopped walking. Her lower lip trembled. "Then he . . . he slapped me. Said I didn't have no right to be dreamin' dreams. He wanted to know where the gold was, so I told him you was holdin' it till it could go in the bank and that was that. Then he got even madder and stormed off."

Christy put her arm around Ruby Mae. "This has all gotten awfully complicated, hasn't it?"

"Worser than those 'rithmetic problems you gave us to figure."

Mr. Halliday was emerging from the shed as they approached. He was wearing a black apron. In his hand was a large photograph.

"We brung you some fresh cookies," Ruby Mae said.

"Wonderful! I'll trade you." Mr. Halliday handed the photograph to Ruby Mae. She passed him the cookies

"You're just in time to see my latest effort," he said. He bit into a cookie. "Wonderful cookie. My compliments to the chef."

Ruby Mae squinted at the photo. "It's a creek," she said. "Looks like Dead Man's."

"So? What do you think?"

Ruby Mae shrugged. "I don't mean to be hurtful, but it just kinda looks like a bunch of water to me."

"I think it's lovely, Mr. Halliday," Christy said quickly.

Mr. Halliday stroked his beard. "Thank you, Christy. But I've already appointed Ruby Mae as my primary critic. She has a wonderful eye."

"*Two* good eyes," Ruby Mae said.

"I stand corrected." Mr. Halliday took the photo and held it out at arm's length, gazing at it critically. "What's wrong with it, Ruby Mae?"

She leaned against the shed, lips pursed. "I don't rightly know. I guess it's just water. Your tree picture, that had the mountain and the sky, all wrapped up together."

"So it's the composition you have trouble with. Not the subject."

"What do I know?" Ruby Mae said irritably. "I ain't no expert."

"Of course you are. You know the beauty of these mountains as well as anyone. And if I'm not getting it on film, well then, I'm not really doing my job, am I?" Mr. Halliday took the photo into the shed, then returned. "Ah well, I shall have to try again. It's a hard task, capturing the riches of this place for posterity. Perhaps it can't be done."

"Ain't no more riches," Ruby Mae said. Christy was surprised at her angry tone. "I keep tellin' everybody, we done found all the riches there was. It was just plumb lucky, is all."

Mr. Halliday looked at her thoughtfully. "I wasn't referring to those riches, actually."

"What, then?"

"I was talking about the incredible beauty of the evergreen trees. The way the sun paints the garden with gold in the morning. The way the warblers argue in the woods."

"Shucks," Ruby Mae said. "That ain't riches. That's just the way the mountains is."

"Exactly." Mr. Halliday reached for another cookie. "There's something else, too. The way the people here love the mountains. And each other. You can't put a price on that."

"You didn't see too much of that at church today," Christy said with a rueful smile.

"Sure I did. By the time everything settled down and the congregation got to singing hymns and clapping and carrying on. I saw it, all right. There was so much love in that room I thought the roof might just pop right off." Mr. Halliday looked at Ruby Mae. "That's all part of the composition, don't you suppose?"

Ruby Mae rolled her eyes. "Beggin' your pardon, Mr. Halliday. But you talk in pure riddles sometimes."

He laughed. "I like you, Ruby Mae Morrison. You speak your mind."

"Well, my mind says I need to go help Miss Ida clean up. But before I go, I was wonderin' . . ." Ruby Mae glanced at Christy nervously.

"Wondering?" Mr. Halliday repeated.

"Well, I know Miz Christy gave that catalog back to you and all . . . but I was wonderin' if I could tear out one tiny little picture in it."

"I wouldn't mind at all. Let me go get the catalog. It's in the shed."

Ruby Mae gave Christy a sheepish smile. "I promise it ain't for makin' anybody feel bad, Miz Christy."

"Just remember what we talked about, all right?"

Mr. Halliday returned with the catalog. "There you go."

"Miss Ida has some sewing scissors," Ruby Mae said. "I promise I'll be right careful."

"Bring it back when you're done," Christy called as Ruby Mae dashed off. She smiled at Mr. Halliday. "I think she's a little preoccupied by all the commotion lately."

"Indeed. Who wouldn't be?"

"Well, I'll let you get back to your work. But I wanted to ask you something first. David and I were wondering if you ever take photographs of people anymore."

"Not really." Mr. Halliday gave a wistful smile. "I suppose I've seen all I need to see of people. Through the lens of my camera, at least."

"We were just thinking . . . well, that a photograph of the congregation—everybody, all together—might help the people here see themselves differently. As a whole, a group. Although I doubt we could even begin to afford such a thing."

"That's one photo I'd be happy to take."

"How much . . ."

"I've been paid in shillings and pennies and

moonshine and gold nuggets," Mr. Halliday said. He stared past Christy at the green mountains surrounding the mission. "But you've already paid me more than I deserve with your hospitality. If anything, I owe you. I fear I've rather complicated lives here."

"You? But how?"

"Oh, the catalog . . . and other things," Mr. Halliday said vaguely. "You tell the reverend I'd be delighted to take a picture of the people of Cutter Gap. I only hope I can do them justice." He gave a sad smile. "After all, I can't even seem to photograph a simple creek."

❧ Fourteen ❧

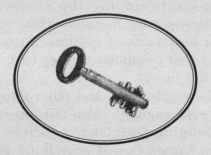

That evening, Christy went to her bedroom and closed the door. It was a beautiful night, warm and perfumed with flowers. A full moon lit her room like a golden lamp. She looked out the window and sighed. Mr. Halliday was right. Such beauty!

She walked to her bed and slipped her hand under her mattress. The key was there, just where she'd left it.

Slowly, Christy unlocked her trunk. She opened the jewelry box. The gold inside looked dull in the moonlight. How could a handful of rocks hold such power? The power to make grown men fight and young girls cry. The power to split families and change lives forever.

Where had it come from, and why was it here? Was it just "plumb lucky," as Ruby Mae

had said? Or did this gold belong to someone
. . . perhaps someone right here in Cutter Gap?

Again she went over her conversation with
Mr. Halliday that afternoon by the shed. "I
fear I've rather complicated lives here," he'd
said. What had he meant by that?

He'd talked today of having been paid in
gold. And he'd taken photographs near the
very creek where Ruby Mae and her friends
had found the nuggets.

Suddenly, she remembered the white piece
of cloth Ruby Mae had been holding when
Christy and Doctor MacNeill had confronted
Lundy. It had looked like a handkerchief.

Like one of Mr. Halliday's handkerchiefs.

But why, if the gold belonged to him and
he'd lost it, hadn't he told them the truth?

And could it be that Ruby Mae had the
same suspicions?

Christy put away the gold. She locked her
trunk and hid the key. Then she pulled out
her diary and began to write.

*What if my instincts are right? What if the
gold that filled the girls with such hope—and this
community with such anger—really belongs to Mr.
Halliday? He's such a kind man. I doubt he'll ever
be able to bring himself to say anything. But if
Ruby Mae and the other girls know this gold isn't
just the result of luck . . . If they know that their*

gold really belongs to someone else, and that they're taking advantage of his kindness, they'll never be able to live with themselves. The question is, am I right? And if I am, how can I find a way to reach the girls before Mr. Halliday leaves forever?

"Lots of children missin' today," Clara commented on Monday morning as she took her seat next to Ruby Mae and Bessie.

"Out gold-huntin'," Bessie said. "Pa said everybody from here to Asheville's heard about it by now. Said he wished he had some pickaxes and shovels to sell."

"At least Lundy ain't here," Ruby Mae muttered. "Probably scared to show his face." She turned to check the door. "Mountie O'Teale come yet?"

"Why are you so all-fired interested in Mountie all of a sudden?" Bessie asked.

"No reason."

The girls watched as more children took their seats.

"Am I crazy," Clara whispered, "or are we sittin' all by ourselves? How come everybody else is off in other rows?"

Bessie scanned the room. "You'd think we had the pox!"

"They're just treatin' us like royalty, is all," Ruby Mae said.

A few minutes later, Mountie entered the schoolroom. Ruby Mae leapt from her seat and pulled the little girl aside.

"I got something to show you," Ruby Mae said excitedly.

"Don't care," Mountie said softly. "I know I ain't no princess, but that's all right. 'Cause I got my 'magination. Teacher said."

Ruby Mae pulled a slip of paper from the pocket of her dress. "Here. This is to help your imagination. For when it gets tuckered out and needs some help rememberin'."

Mountie stared at the little piece of paper. Her mouth worked, but no sound came out. "I-it's my dolly!" she whispered.

"Mr. Halliday let me cut her out of the catalog."

"Can I keep hold of this for a little while?"

"You can keep it, Mountie. It's for you to have." Ruby Mae looked away. "I know she ain't a real dolly, but she's easier to carry."

"Th-thank you, Ruby Mae!" Mountie whispered.

Ruby Mae had never seen Mountie grin so wide. "Shucks, Mountie. Ain't nothin' much," she muttered. Quickly she ran back to her seat.

"What was that about?" Bessie asked.

"Nothin'. Just 'cause we're princesses don't mean I can't talk to the common folk, do it?"

"Don't get all riled," Bessie said. "You ain't

mad at me 'cause our pas was beatin' up on each other in church, are you?"

"Naw," Ruby Mae gave a short laugh. "You mad at me?"

Bessie giggled. "Naw. Can't help it if'n the grownups act like kids. It's a good thing we can act proper-like."

Ruby Mae glanced back over her shoulder. Mountie was hugging the little piece of paper to her chest as if it were a real doll. "Yep," Ruby Mae said softly. "It's a good thing we can act proper-like."

❧ Fifteen ❧

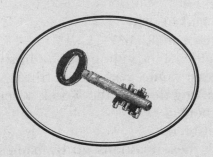

Instead of reading from a book today," Christy said later that morning, "I thought maybe I'd tell you a story."

Her announcement was met with enthusiastic applause. Even the older children loved it when she told stories. Fairy tales, myths, mysteries—it didn't matter what. She wasn't sure if it was her storytelling ability, or the fact that they preferred just about anything to the prospect of another arithmetic or spelling lesson.

Christy sat on the edge of her desk. The children pulled their desks and chairs closer. She couldn't help noticing that Ruby Mae, Bessie, and Clara were sitting apart from the others. She wondered if it was their doing, or if the other children were keeping their distance.

"This is the story of three fair maidens," Christy began.

"Teacher?"

"Yes, Little Burl?"

"What's a maiden?"

"A maiden is a young girl." Christy cleared her throat. "One day, these three maidens were walking through the woods when they—"

"Teacher?"

"Yes, Creed."

"Don't these maidens go by names?"

"That's a very good question, Creed. Let's see. Their names were Lucinda, Drusilda, and—"

"Pearl!" Creed exclaimed.

"Excuse me?"

"I'm right partial to Pearl, Teacher. If'n it don't get in the way of your storytellin'."

"Pearl it is." Christy smiled to herself. She'd long since learned that with the aid of her students, a ten-minute story could take an hour.

"As I was saying, Lucinda, Drusilda, and Pearl were walking through the woods on a bright summer day when suddenly the air was filled with the most beautiful sound their ears had ever heard. 'It sounds like the first call of birds in the morning,' said Lucinda. 'It sounds like a church bell on Christmas morning,' said Drusilda. 'It sounds like angels singing,' said Pearl."

"What was the sound, Teacher?" Mountie asked shyly.

"Well, the maidens didn't know for sure, Mountie," Christy said. Then she lowered her voice to a whisper. "Very carefully the maidens crept to the clearing that seemed to be the source of the wonderful sound. But Pearl tripped on a root—she had very large feet—and suddenly the sound vanished. All was still."

Christy glanced over at Ruby Mae and her friends. They were listening as attentively as the other children—maybe even more so.

"Well, the maidens went to the clearing. They saw footprints leading away into the woods. They saw a campfire, too, the embers still glowing from the night before. And next to the campfire, what do you think they saw?"

"A family of three bears?" Creed ventured.

"Well, no, Creed, that's another story. What they saw was a tiny silver flute. That's a long, thin tube with holes in it. It's a kind of musical instrument, just like the dulcimer Clara's father likes to play."

"Or like the piano over to the mission house that Wraight plays on?" Lizette asked.

"Exactly," Christy said, grinning. It was no secret that Lizette and Wraight Holt were "sweethearts," as the children put it.

Christy paused for a moment, considering

where to take her story. She was making it up as she went along, and she wanted to be sure she got her point across to three members of the audience in particular.

"Well, the maidens gave some serious thought to this flute," she continued. "'Maybe we should leave it,' Drusilda said. 'After all, it doesn't really belong to us. Maybe the music-maker was so frightened he left this behind. Or maybe he left it for us out of the kindness of his heart.' But Pearl was the leader of the group, and she said, 'No, if we found it, it's ours, fair and square.' So she picked up that silver flute and she put it in her pocket and off the maidens set for home."

"So then they played songs on it, Teacher?" George O'Teale asked.

"Well, that's the thing, George. Drusilda tried, and Lucinda tried, and Pearl tried. They blew on that flute till their faces were purple, but the only thing that came out was the most dreadful noise. A noise like a hungry hog and a balking mule and a howling hound all mixed up together. The maidens had to wear earplugs day and night while they tried to make that sweet music they'd discovered in the woods. But you know what?"

Christy looked over at Ruby Mae. She was staring at the ceiling with a strange, unhappy gaze, her mouth set in a frown.

"The maidens couldn't make the silver flute

play because it wasn't theirs. They'd taken something that didn't belong to them, and because of that, there was no joy in it." Christy paused. "Finally, in frustration, the maidens took the silver flute back to the clearing in the woods. Day after day they waited patiently, hidden in the trees, far enough away so the music maker wouldn't be afraid. On the last day, when they were just about ready to give up, what do you think happened?"

"Music!" George cried, and the other children laughed.

"Exactly, George. Music happened. The owner of the flute returned, and made the sweetest, most joyous, most angelic music the maidens had ever heard, even more beautiful than before."

"And is that the end, Teacher?" Creed asked.

"That's the end, Creed."

"Ain't no point to this story," Ruby Mae said darkly, speaking up for the first time. "They found the flute. They coulda kept it."

"But it weren't rightfully theirs," Clara said softly. "So they couldn't make music. You see, Ruby Mae?"

"Tell us another one, Teacher!" Creed urged.

"And make this one have a better ending," Ruby Mae muttered.

"I'm tellin' you, Ruby Mae," Clara insisted during the dinner spell that noon, "Miz Christy was tryin' to learn us a lesson. We're the three maidens, don't you see? And she's sayin' if the gold don't rightly belong to us, maybe we should give it back to the person it does belong to."

Ruby Mae lay back on the springy lawn, chewing on a blade of grass. "First off, we don't know who it belongs to. And second, who's to say we won't do more good with it than he would?"

"He," Bessie repeated. "You mean Mr. Halliday."

"I don't mean anyone!" Ruby Mae shot back.

"That was his handkerchief by the bank," Bessie reminded her.

Clara set her bread aside and brushed the crumbs off her dress. "I think we need to have an official-like meetin' of The Princess Club. Right here and now. We need to take a vote."

Ruby Mae sat up. "Vote on what?"

"On givin' back the gold," Clara whispered harshly. "What do you think? All for it, raise your hands."

Bessie's hand shot into the air. So did Clara's.

Ruby Mae couldn't believe her eyes. "Are you crazy? What about your education? What

94

about your frilly dresses? Have you forgotten all our plans?"

"Don't matter havin' plans," Clara said, "if you got no friends to share them with."

"Besides," Bessie added, "I'm tired of all the fussin' and feudin'. Like with my pa and your pa. Craziness, all of it." She gave an embarrassed smile. "And to tell you the truth, it just don't feel right, spendin' money that ain't rightfully ours. Even if we haven't *really* spent any of it yet."

"But . . ." Ruby Mae threw up her hands in exasperation. "What's got into you two? Some silly story about a flute, and all of a sudden you want to give up your future? We all agreed that if'n the money was Mr. Halliday's, he shoulda owned up to it."

Bessie and Clara just stared at her blankly. "We took a vote, Ruby Mae," Clara said. "Fair and square."

"All right, then," Ruby Mae said. "How about this? How about we give it a day to sink in? You know, think about it longer. You love to think about things, Clara. You can fret over this for another day for sure. Then, we'll vote again tomorrow. And whatever the club decides, that's what we'll do."

Clara chewed on a thumbnail. "Well, I s'pose one more day wouldn't hurt. But that's all."

"Deal?" Ruby Mae turned to Bessie.

"I don't have to think any more on it, do I?" Bessie asked. "My head already hurts from all this frettin'."

"No, Bessie. You don't have to." Ruby Mae stood, arms crossed over her chest. "Then we're decided. Tomorrow we vote. Till then, no matter what, the gold's still ours."

✌ Sixteen ✌

"May I be excused?" Ruby Mae asked at dinner that evening.

"I suppose," Christy said. "But you barely touched your chicken."

"Just ain't hungry, I reckon. It was fine chicken, though, Miss Ida."

"I'll second that," Mr. Halliday said heartily.

"As a matter of fact," the preacher said, "I'll eat that last piece on your plate, Ruby Mae. Unless you'd like it, Mr. Halliday."

"All yours, Reverend. Eat any more, and I'll burst."

Ruby Mae pushed back her chair and carried her dishes to the sink in the kitchen. She slipped upstairs without a sound.

At the top of the stairs, she paused in front of Miz Christy's room. Her heart was hammering inside her chest.

All afternoon, she'd known she was going to end up in this spot. But now that she was really here, she wasn't sure if she should go through with her plan.

Downstairs, the grownups were laughing and talking. Mr. Halliday had spent the whole dinner talking about his trips to faraway places. He'd even told them how he'd had dinner at the White House after he took the President's photograph. A fine meal, he'd said, but not as fine as Miss Ida's fried chicken.

The more he had talked, the more Ruby Mae had realized he didn't need the gold, even if it *was* really his. He was a man with a camera and a fancy catalog and lots of white handkerchiefs and a gold pocket watch. What did a little gold matter to him? If he needed more money, he could always take more pictures of fancy people.

With trembling fingers, Ruby Mae eased open Miz Christy's door and slipped into her bedroom. The setting sun had turned everything golden. The room smelled of lilac talcum powder, the way Miz Christy always did. Unlike Ruby Mae's room, everything was in its place, neat as a pin.

On the dresser was a picture of Miz Christy's family, smiling at the camera. Ruby Mae looked at it. Even though she'd seen it a hundred times before, tears suddenly spilled down her cheeks.

Miz Christy had a happy family. So did Bessie and Clara.

They could talk all they wanted about silver flutes and such, but the gold meant far more to Ruby Mae. She didn't have anyone she could really depend on. She didn't have the kind of family they did.

Sure, she'd talked about horses and mansions and dozens of kids. But what she truly wanted was a way to feel safe. What if Miss Alice and the preacher decided they couldn't let her stay at the mission any longer? What if her pa and ma wouldn't take her back in? Her pa had kicked her out once already. Where would she go then?

Ruby Mae wanted this gold. She wanted it just the way Mountie wanted that silly doll. Only worse.

She wiped away her tears with the back of her hand. She hated all this thinking. How did Clara stand it?

Taking a deep breath, Ruby Mae ran over to Miz Christy's bed, slipped her hand under the mattress, and found the trunk key. It took two tries to get it open, but finally the lock clicked.

Carefully, Ruby Mae opened the wooden jewelry box. There it was. Hope.

She scooped up all the nuggets and put them in her pocket. Her hands were shaking like leaves in the wind. Just as she started to lock the trunk, she heard voices on the stairway.

Her heart leapt into her throat. Leaving the key in the lock, Ruby Mae slid under Miz Christy's bed just as the door opened.

Miz Christy took another step, and another. Ruby Mae could see her teacher's shoes. They were close enough to touch. She feared she would scream from the awful waiting.

"That's funny," Miz Christy murmured. "I could have sworn I heard something."

"Coming?" the preacher called from downstairs.

"Just a minute, David. I'm getting my shawl. It's cool tonight."

Step. Step. Ruby Mae heard a drawer slide open. Step. Step. Step.

The door closed.

For the first time in what seemed like hours, Ruby Mae took a calming breath. She waited under the bed a long time, until, through the window, she heard the sound of Miz Christy and the preacher talking outside in the yard.

Ruby Mae eased her way out from under the bed. Her pocket bulged. There was something she needed to do, but what? Her head was still buzzing with fear.

Find a place to hide her gold, maybe that was it. Somewhere in her room where no one, not even nosy Miss Ida, would ever find it. Stuffed deep in her feather pillow, maybe.

Ruby Mae went to the door and peeked outside. It was safe.

She headed for her room, whistling softly.

A tune as pretty, she thought, as anything you might hear on a silver flute.

*   *   *

That night, Christy couldn't sleep. Maybe it was the full moon, lighting up the room. Or maybe it was the fact that David had thought he'd heard noises that evening around the mission house. He and Mr. Halliday had done a thorough search and hadn't found a thing, but still, it was hard to relax with the gold right here in her room.

It was a relief to know that Mr. Halliday was staying here. And David was in his bunkhouse, close enough to come if help were needed.

She went to the window and listened. Crickets thrummed noisily. A branch cracked. An owl hooted, soft and low: *HOO-HOO-HOO-HOOOOO*.

Nothing. She was just jumpy. She closed her window and returned to bed. But as she pulled the sheets over her, something glimmering in the moonlight caught her eye.

Her key. The key to her trunk.

For a brief moment, she thought maybe she'd left it in the trunk latch by accident. But no, she distinctly remembered putting it under the mattress.

Christy rushed over to the trunk and opened it. The jewelry box was in its usual place. But when she opened it, just as she'd feared, the gold was gone. Not a nugget was left.

With a sigh, Christy sat on her bed, clutching the key. Who knew about the key? Miss Alice, David, Neil, Miss Ida.

And Ruby Mae.

No. She couldn't let herself think that way. Ruby Mae wouldn't, she couldn't . . .

Perhaps someone else had found out about the trunk. Rummaged through her room. Found the key.

But Miss Ida was almost always here. It didn't seem very likely.

Still, the alternative was more than Christy could bear to think about.

With a cold feeling in the pit of her stomach, Christy tiptoed to Ruby Mae's room. Gently she knocked on the door. When there was no answer, Christy eased it open a few inches.

Ruby Mae lay there asleep, snoring lightly. Asleep like this, she had the face of an angel.

Christy closed the door. She was going to try to remember that angelic face. And she was going to try very hard to think of some other way the gold might have disappeared.

❧ Seventeen ❧

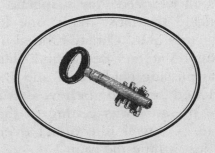

Penny for your thoughts."

Christy looked up in surprise. Neil was standing in the doorway of the classroom, holding another bouquet of violets.

He handed them to her. "Not wilted this time. I'm improving."

"Thank you, Neil. They're lovely."

He leaned on the edge of her desk. "You looked about a million miles away just now."

"I was. I let school out half an hour ago, and I've been sitting here ever since."

"No problems with Lundy, I hope," he said, clearly worried.

"No. He hasn't shown up for school since the incident at the creek. From what I understand, he's probably out prospecting. A lot of the children are."

"What is it, then?" Neil touched her hand tenderly.

"It's the gold. It's been stolen. Right out of my trunk."

"That's all we need. Any suspects?"

"I'm afraid the most likely one has very red, very curly hair." Christy rubbed her eyes. "I told Ruby Mae and Bessie and Clara today about the missing gold. Clara and Bessie almost seemed relieved, believe it or not. I think the pressure was getting to them. But Ruby Mae . . . well, she didn't even blink. She was just a little *too* calm."

"Maybe she didn't take it."

"Maybe. But I can't see who else could have."

"Give her some time. Maybe she'll ''fess up' all on her own."

Christy went to the blackboard and started to erase the day's work. "Who'd have ever dreamed a handful of rocks could be so much trouble?"

"That's what they said in 1849 in California."

"Well, we're having our own Gold Rush of 1912." She sighed. "What am I going to do, Neil?"

He gave her a hug. "Pass me an eraser," he said.

~ ~ ~

"This here," Clara said that same afternoon, "is the last official meeting of The Princess Club. What with us not being princesses no more."

Ruby Mae sat on a bale of hay near the stable. The three girls had already fed Prince, Old Theo, Goldie, and Clancy. Now they were watching the animals munch contently on fresh grain and hay.

"Clancy looks to be gettin' much better," Ruby Mae said. "I wonder if'n Mr. Halliday will be movin' on soon. You think?"

"Ruby Mae!" Bessie cried. "You sure are takin' the news about the gold awful well. We ain't princesses anymore. Don't that bother you?"

"Sure it bothers me," Ruby Mae said quickly. "But ain't nothin' we can do about it."

"Still," Clara pressed, "don't you wonder who took it? Right out from under Miz Christy's nose like that? Who coulda done such a thing?"

Ruby Mae stroked Prince's warm, silky coat. She could feel her face heating up. Was Clara looking at her funny? Or was Ruby Mae's guilt getting the better of her?

"Anybody could have sneaked into the mission house," she said. "Ain't like it's locked up or nothin'."

"Still, they would have had to know where to look," Clara persisted.

"Easy enough to figure out where it was hidden," Ruby Mae pointed out. "There's only one thing with a lock on it in that whole house."

"But then they had to find the key," Bessie added.

"What does it matter?" Ruby Mae blurted. "Me, I'm plumb tuckered out, talking about that gold. If'n we ain't goin' to be princesses no more, let's just start actin' like plain ol' regular people!"

"Ruby Mae!" Bessie grabbed her by the arm. "Hush! Look, over yonder!"

Bessie pointed a trembling finger at a stand of nearby trees. There stood Lundy Taylor. In the crook of his arm was a long hunting rifle.

Bessie gulped. "H-he's got himself a gun!"

"Don't pay him no never mind," Ruby Mae said. "He's probably just out huntin' squirrels."

Suddenly, as quickly as he'd appeared, Lundy vanished into the woods.

"See?" Ruby Mae said. "Don't mean nothin'."

"Still and all," Bessie said, breathing a sigh of relief, "I'm just as glad to be rid of that gold. I didn't need the likes of Lundy after me the rest of my days!"

"Yep," Ruby Mae said, frowning. "I s'pose maybe you're right about that."

~ ~ ~

I thought I'd reached Ruby Mae.

Christy wrote in her diary that night. She paused, pen in hand, when she heard a howl coming from far off on the mountain. The woods were full of noises tonight. Even more than usual.

She turned to a fresh page.

Neil says to give it time, but how much time can I give it? Mr. Halliday will be leaving soon, and I'm more convinced than ever that the gold is his. But if I push Ruby Mae, I'm afraid she'll deny what I'm all too certain is the truth: she took the gold. I suppose all I can do is pray. Perhaps the answer will come to me if I am patient.

When she finally set her diary aside and tried to sleep, Christy tossed and turned, just as she had the previous night. Every now and then she awoke to a sound from the outside. But eventually, she somehow managed to fall asleep again.

Her dreams were full of flutes made of silver and red-haired angels . . . There was something cold in her dreams, too, something cold, pressed against her temple. There were people with her, but these weren't red-haired angels anymore. These people were dangerous. These people meant her harm . . .

Something clicked, like the sound of a rifle being cocked.

Christy's eyes flew open. In the milky moonlight, she could see them plainly—Lundy Taylor and his father, Bird's-Eye. Each one had a gun.

And they were both pointed straight at her.

❧ Eighteen ❧

"Tell us where the gold be," snapped Bird's-Eye, a grizzled man with a permanent scowl. "If'n you do, we won't have to shoot you, Teacher-gal."

Slowly Christy sat up, trying to get her bearings. Miss Ida and Mr. Halliday were in rooms at the far end of the house. Only Ruby Mae's room was nearby. Christy could scream, but who knew what Bird's-Eye would do? She could smell the moonshine on his breath.

This wasn't the first time she'd faced down this man's gun. She knew better than to take him lightly.

Lundy cocked his gun. He jerked it at her. "We knows it's hid in here. So you might as well come clean."

Both men, Christy noticed, were whispering. That meant they didn't want to face Mr.

Halliday and David. They just wanted the gold.

Well, she only had one choice. Tell them the truth.

"I don't have it," Christy said, as calmly as she could.

"Don't go lyin' to us, Teacher-gal. 'Thou shalt not lie.' Ain't that one o' your rules? We knows it's here."

"Gotta be," Lundy said. "That day by the creek, you said it was all locked up. That means you know where it is. And I figger it's gotta be here at the mission house."

"I'm telling you, I don't have it."

"Prove it."

"Fine." Christy went to the trunk and unlocked it. She pulled out her jewelry box. Her hands were trembling as she opened it.

"This is where the gold was hidden. But somebody stole it yesterday. I—I don't know who."

Lundy shoved the gun against her back. "You got it hid somewheres else."

"I'm telling you the truth, Lundy."

"Liar!" Bird's-Eye raised his hand to strike her.

"If I call out, I'll wake everyone in the house," Christy said calmly. "And . . . and Mr. Halliday has a gun." She wasn't sure if that was true or not. But she certainly hoped it was.

"I hit you hard enough, Teacher-gal, and

you won't be able to scream," Bird's Eye growled. "I oughta—"

"No!" a small voice cried.

Christy spun around.

Ruby Mae stood in the doorway in her cotton nightgown. She was clutching her feather pillow to her chest. She rushed over and grabbed at Bird's-Eye's arm with her free hand.

"Let her be, Mr. Taylor," she whispered. "I know where the gold is."

Bird's-Eye and Lundy exchanged a wary glance. "I'm waitin'," Lundy said, jerking his gun at Christy.

Tears flowed down Ruby Mae's face. Frantically, she began digging into her pillow. Feathers floated everywhere as she searched.

"This better not be no trick," Lundy muttered as he brushed a feather from his face.

"A-choo!" Bird's-Eye sneezed. "If'n this . . . achoo! . . . ain't true, I'll . . . achoo!"

"There!" Ruby Mae cried. She dropped a sock onto the bed.

"Looks like a plain ol' sock to me," Lundy said.

Ruby Mae emptied the sock. Gold nuggets rained onto Christy's quilt.

Lundy's eyes went wide. "So they weren't lyin' about the gold! There it is, plain as day, Pa!"

"Weren't my gold." Ruby Mae looked at

Christy. "It's Mr. Halliday's, I'm pretty sure. I shoulda told him I thought it was his a long time ago. But I was just so darn hopeful . . ." She frowned at Lundy. "And it ain't yours, neither."

Lundy dropped his gun and scooped up the gold into his hands. Bird's-Eye ran to join him.

"Looky here, Pa! We is kings now. Just like they was princesses!"

"I beg to differ with that assessment," came a voice from the hallway.

Mr. Halliday appeared in the doorway. He winked at Christy.

Bird's-Eye went for his gun, but before he could, there was a loud click. Mr. Halliday trained a silver pistol directly on Bird's-Eye's hand.

"Hand the guns to Miss Christy," Mr. Halliday said calmly. "And hand my gold to me."

❧ Nineteen ❧

It's a good thing I'm a light sleeper," Mr. Halliday said.

Everyone was gathered around the kitchen table, drinking the warm milk a sleepy Miss Ida had prepared. David and Miss Alice had been roused in their cabins by all the commotion following Lundy and Bird's-Eye's rapid departure.

"I still can't believe the way Lundy and his pa high-tailed it out of here," Ruby Mae marveled. "They took one look at that pistol and left their rifles behind!"

"I still can't figure out why they didn't try to break in during the day," Christy said, shaking her head. "There are fewer people around."

"But I'm here," Miss Ida said, hands on her hips. She held up a frying pan. "And they know I'm well-armed!"

"One other thing I don't understand, Mr. Halliday," said Miss Alice. "Why didn't you just tell us that the gold was yours?"

Mr. Halliday looked at Ruby Mae. "I suppose I didn't want to dash anyone's dreams. The girls had such high hopes." He shrugged. "I've seen my share of good fortune. But things didn't turn out exactly as I'd hoped."

"Me neither." Ruby Mae sighed. "I'm right sorry I didn't 'fess up sooner, about figuring out who the gold belonged to. I pretty much put two and two together—that makes four, by the way!" she added, smiling at Christy. "But I wanted that gold more 'n I wanted to get it to its rightful owner. And look at what it got me. When I think how Lundy and Bird's-Eye might have hurt you, Miz Christy, I just want to up and die. I'm truly sorry."

"I accept your apology, Ruby Mae," Christy said. She reached across the table and squeezed Ruby Mae's hand.

"As do I," said Mr. Halliday. "And I happen to know a way you can make it up to me. I want you to be sure that everybody in Cutter Gap shows up for church this Sunday."

"I wouldn't mind that myself," David said with a chuckle.

"How come?" Ruby Mae asked.

"We've got a photograph to take, young lady. And we want to be sure we get the composition just right."

The following Monday, Mr. Halliday emerged from the shed. He handed a photograph to Ruby Mae.

"Before you give me your opinion," he said, "I want you to remember that it's been awhile since I took a photo of real, live people. Mountains sit still. Babies don't."

Ruby Mae studied the black and white photograph. There, in front of the church, were the residents of Cutter Gap. They stood stiffly, most barefoot. Some people smiled. Most did not.

Granny O'Teale was in the front row, leaning on her cane. Little Mountie stood beside her, clutching her hand. The preacher, Miz Alice, Miz Ida, and Miz Christy were there. Doc MacNeil was scowling at the camera in that way he had, looking gruffer than he really was.

Ruby Mae's eyes fell on three girls, clumped together at the end of a row. They were sharing a smile between them, as if they knew a secret. They looked proud and silly and happy, all at once.

If you squinted just right and didn't think too hard, they even looked a tiny bit like princesses.

"Well," Mr. Halliday said hopefully, "what do you think?"

"I think," said Ruby Mae with a grateful smile, "that the composition is just about perfect."

———

Early the next morning, Ruby Mae and her friends watched as Mr. Halliday packed up Clancy and prepared to leave.

"Don't forget these sandwiches I packed," Miz Ida said, tucking them into Mr. Halliday's knapsack. "And there's fried chicken, too."

"Ida, you are too kind," Mr. Halliday said. He kissed her hand and Miz Ida blushed.

"Where are you headed now?" Christy asked.

"Well, I'm starting toward El Pano. David tells me the road is more or less clear. And I've got some business to attend to there. Banking business, actually."

For a brief moment, Ruby Mae felt a sense of loss of her gold—her gold that was really Mr. Halliday's gold. He was going to put it in the bank, of course. Well, that was only natural. It needed safe-keeping. And it wasn't hers to worry about, anyway. Not anymore.

"I'm opening up a fund there," Mr. Halliday continued as he adjusted the pack on Clancy's back.

"Oh?" Miz Christy asked.

"An education fund, actually. You might be interested in it. It's for the children of Cutter Gap. I'm calling it the Princess Fund."

"For all us children?" Ruby Mae cried. "For us to go to college and such?"

Mr. Halliday nodded. "I'll be adding to it from time to time, as I can."

"You're a wonderful man, Mr. Halliday." Christy gave him a hug.

"We're most grateful," David added.

"You know what the Bible says—'God loveth a cheerful giver.' It's easier to part with money than you might imagine. There are many things worth more than gold. Friends, for example. Which reminds me."

Out of his pocket, Mr. Halliday pulled three white handkerchiefs, each knotted at the top. He handed one to Ruby Mae, one to Bessie, and one to Clara.

"A handkerchief?" Bessie asked, brow knitted.

"There's some gold dust in each of these," Mr. Halliday explained. "Not a lot, but perhaps enough to keep those princess dreams alive."

"Real live gold dust?" Bessie breathed.

"Oh, thank you!" Clara cried. "This is the bestest present I ever got!"

But Ruby Mae was silent. She stared at her handkerchief a long time. "I think," she said quietly, "we need to have one last meetin' of The Princess Club before you leave, Mr. Halliday."

He looked puzzled. "All right, then. I can wait."

Ruby Mae pulled her friends aside. A few minutes later, she went back to Mr. Halliday, carrying all three handkerchiefs. "We done had a vote," she said. "We're givin' these back to you, if'n you don't mind."

"But . . . why?" he asked, looking a little disappointed.

"We got somethin' else in mind for that gold," Ruby Mae said with a sly smile. "But we need your help."

❧ Twenty ❧

Five weeks later, on a sweltering afternoon, Ben Pentland, the mailman, arrived at the school. Christy was writing addition problems on the blackboard when he peered in the doorway.

"United States mail, at your service!" he called.

"Thank you, Mr. Pentland," Christy said. "Why don't you just leave the letters on my desk?"

"Can't do that, Miz Christy," he said politely.

"Why is that?"

"Mail ain't for you." Mr. Pentland grinned. He held up a box, wrapped in brown paper and tied with twine.

The children murmured excitedly. "Who's it for, Mr. Pentland?" Ruby Mae asked.

Mr. Pentland pretended to study the box at great length. "Why, it says here it's for none other than a certain Miss Mountie O'Teale!"

Everyone turned to stare at little Mountie. Her face was white. Her mouth hung slightly open. She gulped.

"Can't be," said one of the older boys. "Who would send a package to Mountie?"

"Let's just see about that," said Mr. Pentland. Again he studied the package. "Return address is kind of queer. Says 'Care of P.C., Cutter Gap, Tennessee.' Mountie, you know anybody with the initials P.C.?"

Mountie shook her head, bewildered.

With great flair, Mr. Pentland placed the package on Mountie's desk. "I guess you'll be a-wantin' to open it," he said.

Mountie barely managed a nod. She was trembling with excitement.

"Here, Mountie," Christy said. "I'll cut the strings with my scissors. Then you can open the rest."

When the twine was off, Mountie set about opening the package. The children gathered around in rapt attention. Christie noticed Bessie, Ruby Mae, and Clara standing off to the side, whispering to themselves.

Slowly, carefully, Mountie tore off the brown paper. Inside was a wooden box. George had to help her yank it open.

Layers of white paper came next. Mountie

pulled off each piece as if the paper itself were a gift.

Suddenly, she gasped. Her hand flew to her mouth. For several moments, she didn't move.

"Go on, Mountie," George urged gently.

With the utmost tenderness, Mountie reached into the box and lifted a beautiful doll into her thin arms. She stroked the shiny curls. She touched the lace-trimmed gown. Then she held the doll to her heart and kissed her.

Tears rolled down her face. "It's her," she whispered. "My 'maginary dolly."

Christy wiped away a tear. She heard quiet sobs behind her and turned.

Bessie and Clara and Ruby Mae were grinning from ear to ear, their own faces damp with tears.

Today, Christy thought proudly, *they really are princesses.*

About the Author

Catherine Marshall

With *Christy*, Catherine Marshall LeSourd (1914–1983) created one of the world's most widely read and best-loved classics. Published in 1967, the book spent 39 weeks on the New York Times bestseller list. With an estimated 30 million Americans having read it, *Christy* is now approaching its 90th printing and has sold over eight million copies. Although a novel, *Christy* is in fact a thinly-veiled biography of Catherine's mother, Leonora Wood.

Catherine Marshall LeSourd also authored *A Man Called Peter*, which has sold more than four million copies. It is an American bestseller, portraying the love between a dynamic man and his God, and the tender, romantic love between a man and the girl he married. *Julie* is a powerful, sweeping novel of love and adventure, courage and commitment, tragedy and triumph, in a Pennsylvania town during the Great Depression. Catherine also authored many other devotional books of encouragement.